Crossing Borders
for the Truth

Crossing Borders
for the Truth

WILLIAM R. CHARLESWORTH

RESOURCE *Publications* · Eugene, Oregon

CROSSING BORDERS FOR THE TRUTH

Resource Publications
A Division of Wipf and Stock Publishers
199 W. 8th Ave., Suite 3
Eugene, OR 97401

www.wipfandstock.com

ISBN 13: 978-1-55635-560-8

Manufactured in the U.S.A.

To those who know there
are many borders to cross to
find the truth, but do not try
to cross every one of them.

CONTENTS

Most of the characters and countries in this story are composites of those the author has encountered on his travels. Also, some of the major border episodes reported here have occurred pretty much as described. With several exceptions, specific names of characters have been replaced by general labels such as "Student" and "Mother." Also, specific names of countries have been replaced by such generic labels as "invaded country" or "occupied people." The author's rationale for labeling this way is to avoid strengthening stereotypes about a particular people or country and to emphasize the universality of human behavior and challenging life problems. Also to note, is that this novel includes concepts and findings from published research (in narrative form, of course). Concepts are stressed because this story was written as a variant of academic fiction that deliberately contains important ideas emerging from academic efforts which the author feels should be made available to the reading public.

Much of the information on children's social behavior reported here is based on published research.

INTRODUCTION

THE BORDER OFFICIAL BECAME frustrated and had to stifle his anger. He suspected the traveler whose face glistened with sweat was not telling the truth. The traveler crossed the border into the official's country to discover some truths, which he did, to some extent. But at this moment he was telling a number of white lies to protect some good people, as he explained later to his friends.

Up to this point, he had not given any hint to the official of his real reason for being in his country. And so far, he had successfully maneuvered the official's attention away from his backpack. His concern was that if the official asked him to open the backpack the situation would change for the worse.

Then, without warning, the official stopped the interrogation and said, "You can go." The traveler picked up his backpack and headed for the exit. (one more down . . . now I got to get out of here)

The traveler's name was Richard and what you just read characterized many of his border crossings. Before we report on the first two of many border crossings, however, let me to turn you over to William, Richard's colleague.

"William here: Before I fill you in on Richard, I should introduce myself. I am some years older than Richard and have some experience in military intelligence. I later studied a wide range of subjects at a prominent university, which prepared me well for a lifetime of writing and thinking. Currently, I have a university position and prefer to work in my library at home. Oh, yes; I also keep in contact with my old comrades in intelligence.

As for Richard, he majored in the humanities while in college, and after graduating, enlisted in army intelligence. His experiences were interesting enough to convince him to make intelligence work a career but he later returned to the university when he realized how little he knew

1

about human behavior. He particularly wanted to know why people act in violent and aggressive ways when faced with difficult situations.

While in graduate school, Richard discovered evidence that explained why some young children become violent, aggressive or sociopathic adults. Many case studies suggested that the roots of adult aggression could be traced to elements in the person's childhood history. Even the most vicious war criminals, many experts came to conclude, were not born monsters. Apart from those with serious brain malfunction, the majority of so-called 'monsters' most likely had been innocent children—that is, until something negative happened to them earlier in their lives.

But what actually did happen? And how could one prove scientifically that what did happen was causally responsible for later anti-social behavior? Both questions compelled Richard to seek answers—no matter what the cost.

I hope you continue to follow me while I try to describe two aspects of his search for truth. These aspects may be quite academic but are worth knowing in order to understand Richard better and the task he undertook.

The first has to do with exploring existing data linking anti social behavior to childhood events. The more Richard learned, the more skeptical he became of what experts claimed about the issue. Critics of the existing treatises on the causes behind anti-social behavior noted the causes varied immensely and, on the whole, were so limited in scope that even the best of them provided only a part of the bigger truth. Richard came to conclude that the main reason for this was a dearth of hard facts—those based on direct observation—on each child's early life experiences and the social circumstances surrounding them. To get an answer to these questions, he felt those studying the problem had to make many observations of children in their everyday environments.

Because Richard also came to believe that aggressive behavior was universal—regardless of culture—researchers should make their observations in many countries. This meant he had to get first-hand information in as many different cultures as possible, directly observing children living in difficult conditions.

The second aspect of his research deals with social behavior in general. Richard understood from his own experiences that most social interactions involved satisfying individual needs. When these needs were not met—where basic resources were scarce—social interactions could become complicated and often antagonistic.

Richard believed that learning how to deal with the problem of scarce resources took place early in life. If children did not learn how to engage in peaceful social interactions, pain and frustration could easily lead to violence.

I agree with Richard's views and his appraisal of the scientific task of obtaining the knowledge necessary to answer the two questions. But in my estimation, his idealism is not well served by his research strategy. The methods he uses are more problematic than he realizes. Also, I believe his strategy to travel to places where children are stressed can be dangerous.

But enough of this. Let us now move on with his story."

1

PURE CURIOSITY

THANK YOU, WILLIAM. Now let us get to Richard's first significant border crossing, one initially motivated more by pure curiosity than anything else, which took place before he began focusing solely on the childhood antecedents of adult aggression.

Shortly after Richard arrived in Europe to carry out his post-doctoral research on children, the director of the institute where Richard was to work invited him to an "open house" party for all new researchers.

Two days before the party, however, an unexpected international event occurred: a neighboring country was invaded by a much larger country. Richard's immediate response was to visit the invaded country to see first hand how its citizens were reacting to such an unusual and threatening situation.

Many of his future colleagues whom he met at the party happened to be from the invaded country. As expected, most of them were in a quandary about what they should do—go back immediately, quietly continue their research until the situation changed, or wait, and then if necessary, seek asylum.

Richard immediately saw an opportunity he could not resist. He would go to the invaded country and witness the aftermath. He was certain he could get a visa because he was from a neutral country. He also assumed that the new government was motivated to demonstrate its openness to visitors, and welcome him with open arms.

It then occurred to him that he could also help his new colleagues. When he told them his plan they were delighted. He could carry messages to their families. "Would you be you be so kind?" they asked, "but please keep in mind to put our letters inside the breast pocket of your jacket. There exists an unwritten agreement never to search there. Why? No one knows."

"If it will be no burden," one colleague said, "would you please bring back some research papers, several books, and a typewriter. That would be of great help to us." Richard's answer was, "Of course, of course." (wow . . . they have fast reaction times)

For Richard's troubles, a young researcher offered him a place to stay in the capital city of the invaded country. The researcher's aunt (she went by "Auntie") was now alone in her apartment and would be delighted to have him stay with her. (perfect!)

The day before he left, he was given Auntie's address and a packet of letters that Auntie would help him deliver when he arrived.

As expected, the train station platform was in turmoil. A rush of shouting people—carrying all kinds of suitcases, net bags, bundles of clothing, and sundries—clustered on the train platform.

When the train arrived and the car doors opened, everyone stormed desperately. Most pushed as hard as they could; the elderly gave way patiently, young adults slithered between the unwary, children slid between the packages and suitcases. A few gave up immediately and just waited.

Richard waited and watched. He was the last to board and immediately found himself stuck in the small entrance area at the end of a car. He had to hold his suitcase against his chest because there was no floor space for it. For the first half hour, he was compelled to listen to the clamor of cars on top of the clattering wheels. He liked that sound. (brings back old memories)

Eventually, he made his way to an aisle and rested his suitcase on the window ledge. As night fell, he worked his way to the toilet compartment, an unlikely sanctuary amid the chaos. He locked the door and hoped he would not be interrupted too often. He got some sleep, but woke occasionally because his arms were stiff from holding his suitcase on his lap. At about 5 A.M., he got off his throne, washed his face, and went into the aisle to look out the window. The train began slowing down.

A misty meadow appeared; scattered large oaks, their trunks and branches blackened with morning dew, stood heavily in the moving moisture. There she was, dressed in black, hoeing in her garden, the woman whom Richard often thought about when reading history or seeing photos of war and its aftermath: a gray-haired woman, the silent and eternal hero of civilization. She and thousands of others had their babies, cooked, mended, swept their huts, cared for the sick, knocked off miles of mortar from stones of destroyed buildings, cleared tons of bombing rubble, and in wartime, patiently held aloft photos of missing relatives as trains arrived from the front.

Other than family, neighbors, and church members, few people knew these women existed. The rich and powerful certainly didn't see them, but these women did not care for the wealthy or the important, nor did they trust them. They had their homes, their families and gardens, their prayers and secret thoughts, and their churches. If asked some day about their lives, they would say, "We are satisfied. Yes, life is not easy, but is it any easier for everyone else? Yes, life could have been better but in the end we are all the same—we are all like the earth in the garden and will end up there." (my hero, I salute you)

The train slowed down and began rolling rhythmically into the city that was to be his destination. A long, drawn-out industrial area appeared—mazes of tracks, rusty-brown utility buildings, large metal machine hangers. It was a desolate area but still very functional. Behind it, in the distance, were the roofs and towers of the city.

Then a shiver ran down the back of his neck. They were there—tanks and half-tracks, personnel carriers, ammunition trucks—about twenty of them. Small groups of soldiers stood around smoking and chatting. The local newspaper article on the invasion was standard propaganda: "The invasion was a great success: the army met with no armed resistance, just unruly civilians, mostly young people whom officials said had nothing to do but act like rowdies and block reform. That some were shot was unfortunate, but they should not have intervened. Difficult times require difficult measures." So far, responses from most foreign papers were cautious. No sense stirring things up.

When the train stopped, the passengers rushed off. Richard took his time watching them. He was always transfixed by train stations—the smell of oil and food, the chaotic clangs and grinds, the forever-flowing social scene. Anyone could be there—from peasant to politician. (wonderful)

The city was old and grand, with tasteful, majestic stone buildings, kiosks, small parks, and a magnificent river lined by promenades. (the air . . . what was that smell . . . yes, it is soft coal burning . . . a long time since I smelled it)

He strolled leisurely down the main street and came to a great plaza with a bronze horseman in the middle carrying an immense sword (warriors always get the highest ground). At the foot of the warrior young people milled around, placing flowers, burning candles, and wreaths at the base of the pedestal—one of the quiet moments of the protest.

Richard wandered back to the train station, found a cheap hotel, and checked in. He gave them his passport and held out his hand to retrieve it. "No," they said," tomorrow morning."

"What? I need it now! I do not go anywhere without my passport."

"Sorry sir, those are the rules."

In his room, he fell asleep immediately and awoke to a darkening sky (up and out!). Before he left, he tied a black sewing thread to the lid of his suitcase near the hinge and fastened it to the suitcase proper. (we shall see how inquisitive they are . . . I will carry the letters with me, however)

He went down to the hotel desk and asked for his passport. "It has not been processed yet," the clerk said.

"Oh!" Richard turned around and walked out of the hotel. (security forces do most of their work at night)

He went back to the plaza where hundreds, mostly young people, now clustered. Candles were burning next to photographs of loved ones, presumably those killed during the invasion. In the middle stood a young woman reading something—at first it sounded like a series of names, then what seemed like a poem. She was honoring the heroes of the past along with those just martyred.

He studied the crowd: no sign of the invading forces (smart to stay away . . . let these people vent their frustrations . . . armies do not have to listen to poems . . . only win wars). Then Richard noticed a middle-aged man who did not fit into the crowd. The man was taking keen notice of the protesters—probably registering faces, clothing, any spoken names. (security is always on the job . . . everywhere . . . but ludicrously obvious)

Richard checked his map to find Auntie's address, relieved that she was easy to find—just across the river near the big ridge. He then found a restaurant and had good meal. Afterward, he wandered the city and got lost. He was on an empty street—no pedestrian was to be seen. He noticed for the first time that the streetlights were not lit.

A man appeared. Richard asked him the way to the plaza. The man eagerly gave him directions, then said, "Are you an American?"

"Yes."

"Good. You are our friend. You understand the enemy, right?"

"Yes."

"I hope you tell your friends in America everything you see here."

"I certainly will."

The man reached into his modest briefcase and brought out a white silk handkerchief painted garishly with flowers. "This is a gift for you. I hope when you look at it you will remember us as your friends."

"Thank you, thank you." Richard was very touched and reached for his wallet.

"No sir. We are friends."

The man walked off and Richard headed to the hotel. When he checked his suitcase, the thread was broken.

At about 2:30 A.M., he heard the front door of the hotel slam.

(security coming to check the passports)

He awoke at 6:00 A.M., got his passport, left the hotel, and after a cup of coffee, headed for the bridge. When he crossed the river, he looked for the street sign indicated on his map. (it must be right here at the corner of the bridge street and the street running perpendicular to it . . . but)

"It's not there!" he said out loud. "This map is not correct!"

He walked to another nearby street, still unsure of his bearings. (also wrong . . . what's going on . . . the signs don't look right!)

He stopped an elderly man and asked for directions. The man smiled. "The street signs have been changed around during the invasion to confuse the enemy. Ha, ha. They still don't know their way around here. They don't even understand we played a trick on them. Even when they go home, they will not understand us, our city, or our people." He smiled again. "Now, what address are you looking for?"

Richard showed him the piece of paper Auntie's niece gave him.

"Oh, yes, that is close by. Let me take you there."

The building was a three-story, gray-stone apartment. The outside lobby door was unlocked. A small panel with apartment numbers adjacent to white buttons was tacked to the wall next to the inside door. Richard pushed Auntie's number several times and got no answer. On the fifth push, the lock on the inside door clicked open. (good . . . she is home)

He climbed to the third floor; the stairs creaked with age. The scent was familiar but difficult to describe. At the top a door was open and in the light from the room stood a tall man. He looked in Richard's direction. "She is not here. She told me you were coming. She will be back shortly. Please come in. I heard you ring her place and guessed it was you."

"Yes." Richard introduced himself. The man let Richard in and pointed to the living room.

"Excuse my arrangement," he said. Richard suddenly noticed that the man was blind. He was distinguished, wore a clean, faded blue shirt, an elbow-patched sweater with antler buttons, black trousers, and corduroy slippers. The living room was of the 1920s: dried-out potted plants near a window, old lithographs and sepia photos on the walls, a violin case on top of a vitrine containing many knick knacks. (many memories here)

"Excuse this place. I am never sure how it looks. I am blind."

"Your place looks fine."

"Auntie comes by now and then and keeps it in order."

"Can I help you?"

"Not necessary. I get around okay, just takes me longer. You are here touring our country?"

"Partly. I am a colleague of Auntie's niece."

"Yes, I hear she is abroad doing research."

"Yes."

There was a hurried knock on the door, then Auntie entered a bit out of breath. "Wonderful! You made it! I'm so glad you're here. So much to talk about." (she is one of those eternal women). She shook Richard's hand, thanked her neighbor, and put a small brown paper bag into his hand. "For your afternoon coffee."

"Many thanks," the man smiled. "Now go and tell your stories."

By the next afternoon Richard had learned much. Before the invasion, the country was in turmoil. Many felt the government had become corrupt. A majority of the young people wanted greater freedom, but the government was propped up by the country that decided to invade. The invaders knew that international disapproval would be great, but what could the world do? Ask an overwhelming army to return home? Within weeks, a vast sea of tanks massed outside the border—"on maneuvers," officials insisted. To everyone's surprise, the tanks moved in without warning.

"So now here we are," Auntie continued, "back to the bad days of long ago. My neighbor, the man you met, was a professor of classical languages, but also quite critical of our government. The officials arrested him and sent him to prison. They beat him so badly he eventually lost his sight, so they released him from prison. They did not wish to feed him, and since he was no longer dangerous, they sent him home. My husband died of typhus in the war and my brother was also arrested several years ago for illegal political activity. He had no trial and was put in prison."

After a long pause, Auntie continued. "Then after he was in prison a short while, I got a . . . excuse me," she wiped her eyes. "I got a package from the prison. It contained his sweater and was soaked in blood. Can you imagine? A month later, I got another package, this time with his shirt, torn and bloody. Can you imagine such barbarians! Then sometime later, I got a note. 'Your brother died in prison trying to escape.' What a lie! But I tell you the truth. You will never hear of this truth in your country. So now you hear it from me. Please tell this to everyone you know when you go back."

She paused and wiped her eyes again. "Enough of that. Now let's have some tea and then I will ask you for a favor."

Tea was gentle, modest, civilized. Richard was touched.

"Now for business," Auntie said, looking directly at Richard. "My hearing aid no longer works well, and I do not know anyone who can fix it. Maybe you can find someone for me. I have difficulty moving about these days. Also, as a visitor, people around here will be helpful to you—more than to me. Many now see me as being different—I can't go into that—or most of them know about my brother and do not want to be seen with me. So I am pretty much isolated here. Oh, I wish my niece were here."

Richard immediately folded his napkin, placed it on the table, then got up and looked down at the carpet (good . . . no crumbs). "I will start looking for someone right now. It will give me a wonderful chance to see your city."

"Yes, it still is a beautiful city with much culture. Go and see it. When you come back, we'll have a good dinner."

It took Richard the rest of the day to find someone who agreed to check out the hearing aid. "It is old and will need some work. Come back in two days," the man told Richard.

On his way back to the apartment, he came to a street that ended at the steps of an enormous cathedral. He went in. It was majestic and very quiet. Several people were kneeling in a pew near the nave. In the distance, at the step leading to the sanctuary, two military officers of the invading forces were talking quietly to each other. Their uniforms were impeccable. One of them was pointing to the altar and saying something. Richard moved closer to eavesdrop.

From out of the gloom of a side chapel, a figure suddenly emerged, muttering loudly. He appeared to be a street laborer. He was dressed in a dirty gray jacket, had large soiled hands, and a small tuft of gray hair. He looked very angry and reeked of alcohol. He walked up to the officers and began yelling at them. The officers looked at him impassively and then turned away, continuing their conversation. The intruder was not to be ignored. He stepped provocatively in front of the two officers and began taunting them (what a brave guy . . . or maybe crazy . . . must be very angry). One of the officers casually put his hand on his pistol and walked away, followed by the other.

Richard worried that his presence may provoke another outburst, walked away, hoping to preempt further tension. The officers slowly walked toward the west end of the nave toward the baptistery. The man followed them, still muttering what sounded like curses. The officers left the church.

Richard felt a sudden urge to talk to the man, about anything—the church, the city, whatever—then invite him out for a drink. But Richard stopped himself. (what the hell are you thinking . . . in his state nothing I say will help . . . hope he sleeps it off)

Two days later, Richard went back to the hearing-aid expert, picked up the device, and took it back to Auntie. She said it was better, but he had a feeling she was not telling him the truth.

2

UNEXPECTED OUTCOME

THE DAY BEFORE HE was to leave, two students arrived; they were old university friends of Auntie's niece. They had a car and were going to visit her at the institute.

"Do you want to go along?" one of them asked.

"Wonderful! I'd be delighted. I can help with the gas."

"Good."

They sat down for dinner and got into a heated discussion about different forms of government, and the use of force versus persuasion in settling international disputes. To Richard's surprise, it became clear that both students were on the side of the invading forces, or at least in favor of their ideological position. (I wonder if Auntie and her niece know this?)

Richard decided to change the discussion's course; one topic followed another, and it wasn't until 2 A.M. that Richard got up from the table and said, "Time to sleep. We have a long day tomorrow."

The next morning, Auntie greeted them smiling. On the sofa in the living room was a pile of folders held together by string, about ten books, a typewriter, a teddy bear, and a plastic bag packed with something or other. In her hand, she held three envelopes containing letters, one for each of them.

"Here are things to take back. My niece will know what to do with them. I am so grateful that you have a car. It makes it so easy," she said smiling again. "Oh, yes, and here is something to eat on the way. You'll get hungry, I am sure."

The students looked at each other. Then they looked at Richard for what he thought was support. He gave them none.

The trip to the border went quietly. The students apparently stayed up drinking after Richard went to sleep, and were now in the mid-process of waking up. They said nothing.

All went well with the passports, but when the officials looked into the back of the car where Richard was sitting, the situation changed.

"What is this? Are all these things yours?" One of the officials asked Richard.

"Not quite," Richard said.

"Please get out. You," the official pointed to Richard, "this is not your car, eh?"

"No."

"You come with me."

Richard got out, taking a quick glance at the others. They were standing outside their car looking very unhappy as two other officials climbed into the car and began emptying its contents onto the street.

Inside the checkpoint station, Richard was taken to a small room painted a sickly yellow. There was a table and two chairs in it.

"Wait here," the official said and left. Richard went to the only window in the room; it had bars on it. He checked the door to the room. It was locked. (now what?)

The official returned. "You, you are American. Why are you with these people?"

"Because they offered me a ride in their car. It is more convenient than riding the train."

"Does any of that stuff in the back of the car and trunk belong to you?"

"Only that green backpack; the rest belongs to colleagues of mine working over there at our institute." He pointed across the border.

"What nationality are these colleagues 'over there'?"

"Many different countries. Some are your nationality."

"Ah. And they need those things?"

"Yes, they need them to conduct their research over there."

"And you?"

"I am also a scientist and came here as a visitor to see your country. I have never visited here before and have always been curious about it. When my colleagues—your people—asked me to bring back things for their research I agreed to do it. You see, scientists cooperate with each other regardless of nationality. I am sure you know that."

"Huh!" the official blurted, then left the room. Five minutes later, he returned. "You may go and so may your friends. But the contents of the car—other than your backpack—stay here."

"What? Why?"

"Your colleagues over there who are from here, their things stay here. They are property of the state."

"But surely not scientific papers and the typewriter." Richard smiled to disarm them. "Surely the state can't use these things."

The official looked at him for second. "I have orders to keep everything that does not belong to visitors." He got up and pointed firmly towards the door.

Richard walked into the waiting room where his two traveling companions were sitting looking very distraught. "Time to go."

(gotta conceal my schadenfreude)

They got up and went to the car. Their suitcases stood next to it.

Richard's backpack was on the back seat.

They continued driving—first on a zig-zag stretch of road with concrete barriers on both side, then up to a steel barrier where an armed guard stood with a portable phone. It rang, he lifted it, listened, nodded his head, put the phone down, shouldered his automatic rifle on its sling (pretty dramatic) and slowly moved the barrier on its hinges away from the car. He then turned to the car and waved the driver to move on. (big man with that gun . . . probably bored to death)

The driver proceeded slowly, seething with anger.

"This is a wonderful country with a wonderful government," Richard laughed.

"Go to hell."

"At least they didn't look in my jacket pocket. How about you? They look in yours?"

No answer.

The official on the other side of the border was smiling broadly,

"They gave you a hard time, eh?" the official said. "They always do. Go ahead. There's a place up ahead you can get a drink."

After the drink, they got gas. Richard paid for both. They arrived at their destination, and as Richard got out the car, he noticed a small piece of paper on the floor of the back seat.

"What is this?" He picked it up and read the note. "Well, well. Guess what is on this paper." He held it up to his companions. They were not interested.

"Hey, you got to hear this." They looked at him impatiently.

"It says, 'Sorry for all this. We have to do it to keep our job. We are still your friends.'"

3

PREROGATIVES OF POWER

Richard was energized by his recent visit. He got a good snapshot of everyday life under stressful conditions. An unwanted foreign military presence will do it every time. But a snapshot was not enough: he wished for a bigger picture and tried to figure ways of getting it. Unexpectedly, his wish was fulfilled.

About ten days after he settled back into his research routine, two totally unrelated things happened within days of each other. His first thought was that it was inconceivable that the two things were unconnected.

First, a university chancellor from the invaded country invited him to give a talk on his research, for a 'modest honorarium.' This was good news because Richard had just written the first draft of a paper hypothesizing the role that surprise played in acquiring and reacting to new knowledge. He could use some critique of his theory before he continued working on it.

The second thing happened while he was walking down the hall (that elderly lady at the end of the hall looks very familiar). The lady turned and saw him. "Hello, Richard, it's been a short time since we last talked." It was Auntie!

"What! What are you doing here?"

"I got a visa to visit my niece and here I am. I can't believe my luck. Actually, I don't think it was luck. The authorities are delighted when an old person leaves their country. They have one less mouth to feed. Also, I am persona non grata so they can kill two birds with one visa. I am sure they hope I stay here, but I won't. My home is there and I am going back, but now I can be with my niece. Isn't that wonderful?"

"Yes, it is. I told your niece about my visit with you; now you can tell her even more about it and what has happened since I last visited. In my recent letter to you I told you the border officials took everything you gave us. Have you gotten any of it back?"

"Yes, I received your letter. No, I got nothing back. It takes them a long time to do anything. Who knows, they may be using the typewriter. According to the state, everything belongs to the state. Ha, ha."

Ten days later, Richard was crossing the border in a rental car. Auntie sat next to him, singing folksongs. Richard decided to cross a different border than the last time, just in case. The trip was pleasant; the sun was out, the landscape was beautiful, and Auntie was doubly pleased about the many bags and packages piled in the back of the car.

Then came the border. Richard felt a slight jolt as an armed guard appeared on the road motioning for Richard to stop. An official appeared, looked into the car, then directed Richard to proceed to two waiting officials.

"Passports please."

Richard handed him his. "And the purpose of your visit?"

"I am speaking at your esteemed university." He pulled out his letter from the chancellor (official invitations are wonderful inventions). The official glanced at its letterhead and handed it back to Richard.

"And your passport, Madam."

Auntie handed hers to Richard, who passed it on to the official.

"And the purpose of your visit?"

"I am not visiting. I am going home."

"Hmm," he said suspiciously. He looked into the back of the car, said something to an official behind him who jotted notes on a clipboard, then walked to the nearby office.

"Wait!" Auntie called out. "My passport!"

The official looked at her impatiently. "I will return it shortly."

The clipboard man approached Richard. "I want to see what you have in the trunk. Open, please." Richard did not know where the trunk latch was, so he got out of the car taking the keys with him. "No, sir, no need to get out." (now he really is suspicious)

"But I have the key."

"I will take it." The official took the key, opened the trunk, then returned the key to Richard. He rummaged through the suitcase—sewing materials, new bed linens, cans of meat, dry foodstuffs, a partially new overcoat, a container of bath powder, a bottle of perfume in a violet package tied with black ribbon. He wrote on his clipboard, opened the rear car door, then took out the suitcases and the seat cushion.

"Will you open your suitcases?"

Richard got out and opened his backpack. The official ran his hands through its contents. Richard then turned to him. "This other one belongs to the lady. I do not open a lady's suitcase."

The official ignored him. "You can open this one."

"No, sir. In my country we do not open a lady's suitcase." Richard held firm. (now let's not be difficult, Richard . . . he can send you right home . . . but not someone with a chancellor's letter)

The official reluctantly opened the suitcase, delicately searched its contents, and shut it carefully.

"Thank you," Richard said, smiling.

The official suppressed a smile and walked away, stopping twice to write something on his clipboard.

The first official appeared and both talked briefly. "Fine. You may go. Oh, by the way," he said to Richard, "do you have the name of the hotel where you will be staying?"

"Actually, I don't. I will find a hotel when I get there. I am sure your city has many wonderful hotels."

"Hmm. It is always wise to book a hotel room before you arrive. Do that next time." He looked curiously at Richard and Auntie, then waved them on.

"Are all your officials as nice as that?" Richard turned to Auntie.

She laughed. "Even nicer. Especially when we bring in things from the outside that make life here more bearable. That saves them from supplying their citizens with those things and helps delay the next revolution. So far, though, they don't take bribes, but that will change after they see how little they are paid."

"You see the big connections," Richard laughed.

The following day, Richard went to the university. The chancellor met him at the door of his spacious office. He was a tall, strongly-built man with an expressionless face—except his eyes, which unnerved Richard. His hair was dyed black, poorly. (his wife should tell him)

"Please come in, come in. We are delighted to have you, especially on such short notice." (I must be a substitute for many refusals)

"As you must know, we—I speak for our new government here—are delighted to renew our contacts with everyone in the international community. The events in the recent past have changed things here and we are now ready to re-establish our friendships with all peaceful countries. As you will see in your stay here, our country is clearly off to a refreshingly new and more democratic beginning."

Richard nodded. (I bet)

"And the topic of your talk?"

"Surprise, knowledge, and mental development. Oh yes, and also beliefs."

"How intriguing." (I bet)

The chancellor called to his secretary in the other room. "Coffee time. I am ready for it. Are you, too, Professor Richard?"

"Yes, I am. You can address me as assistant professor at my talk. I still have a long way to go until I become a professor."

"Of course." (he is disappointed . . . he wanted a bigger fish to visit his pond).

They drank coffee in silence, which Richard found interesting and refreshingly honest.

"Now for your talk. It will begin tomorrow evening at 7 P.M. in our large lecture hall. The psychology department—faculty and students— will be there as well as other interested parties.

"Fine. I am very much looking forward to it."

"Now, if you will excuse me." He got up, nodded, and went to his desk. "I will see you this evening."

The lecture hall was large; the audience was dwarfed by it. Most of the attendees looked like students. What looked like young faculty members sat up front in a supportive cluster; the older-looking were scattered in the back rows, some near the doors for surreptitious escape. (the strategy of the lecture-bored is universal)

After he was introduced as "Professor Richard," Richard approached the lectern. The audience looked in his direction with mixed expressions of interest and fatigue. The chancellor was about five feet from him. (he will see who is paying attention to me and who is not)

"Thank you for inviting me to your world-renowned university." (stay away from anything recent) The chancellor smiled weakly.

"As you know, it is important for scientists—and people in general from the around the world (don't get dramatic)—to have a chance to cross each other's borders, share ideas, and engage in discussions of mutual interest. (you are sounding like a politician)

19

In view of time constraints, I will keep my talk short so we can have ample time for questions and discussion. (a mistake, there could be zero discussion)

As you know, my talk is on surprise and knowledge and how both contribute to mental development and beliefs. I am speaking of the surprise that results when something unexpected happens. This does not include 'startle,' which is usually very sudden and totally unexpected—like a gunshot or a book falling to the floor.

My theory is quite simple. My first assumption is that when we believe something, we believe that something is true because we know it is true. It exists; it is real. It can be verified by others—sometimes, of course, with difficulty. Whether truth in general exists is a matter I will not go into here. Those of you who believe that truth does not exist need not stay any longer to hear my nonsense. I will understand and respect your belief (now for some humor), but I would like to meet you in a pub and give you a chance to change my mind. If you do not change my mind, then I know you believe truth exists."

The audience remained quiet (no sense of humor . . . actually, it wasn't that funny)

"How we get to the belief that something is true can be due to something we have heard or read—from our parents, teachers, textbooks, news media, and of course, our own observations. At any rate, it is important to keep in mind that we are bound by our beliefs. To put it another way: we live within the borders of what we know and believe is true. Whether our beliefs are justified and true is another matter. As you well know, people can easily live around illusions as well. (be very careful dear boy . . . they can easily surmise to what you are referring)

Now, we can't possibly know everything; all knowledge has borders that may be geographical, political, cultural, or ethnic—or even an intrinsic limit to our thinking. Whatever they are, we come to believe and act upon that which is within the borders of our knowledge. An example: for centuries our ancestors believed that the earth was firm and stable; every morning when they got up they could go out and step on it. It was solid, hard. Then, earthquakes changed their views. But no one was sure what caused the earth to quake. Later thinkers came to believe that the earth quaked because of an angry god and still later because heat changes in the earth's core made the surface move up and down. And then, not too long ago, scientists collected new evidence suggesting that the earth's surface was made up of massive plates moving across a molten core. Today, we know this movement is accounted for by tectonic theory.

What brought about these changes to our knowledge of the earth started with skepticism, which was aroused by new observations obtained by people who began to think more deeply about many things, especially those trained in the scientific method who believed in close observations and rational thinking. Their efforts gradually expanded the borders of knowledge. Millions were surprised by their ultimate conclusion, which killed the belief in angry gods. With tectonic theory, a new belief system was born.

Now, let us get to you and me: suppose we become curious for whatever reasons about some phenomenon and decide to explore it—to go to the border of our knowledge and cross over. We may have some idea about what we will discover—because we have a theory. Now suppose we succeed in crossing the border and, 'voila!' We are surprised. Why? Because what we experienced contradicted our expectations.

Suppose, though, we are not surprised. Why? Because we had a good theory that gave us correct expectations—beliefs—of what was beyond the border. We were smart, or maybe just lucky.

Now, surprise may also elicit fear. If so, we may immediately be shocked by what we have observed and return to our old belief. Or surprise may be so satisfying we are motivated to investigate further into what we just discovered. In the process we learn more about it. Our knowledge and our beliefs start to expand.

You're probably not surprised; I suspect you know about this idea already, although you probably don't think about it everyday, as I do. I should also mention how a surprise reaction can reveal whether someone knows something or not. Let me give you an example: a parent comes home and finds a plate lying broken on the kitchen floor. She is sure one of her children broke the plate trying to get to a cookie jar. Her children are out playing. When her children come in, she says, 'Guess what? Our puppy jumped on the table and broke a plate.' She watches the reactions of her two children. One looks and says gravely, 'Bad puppy.' The other child freezes, gets slightly pale, gives a phony smile, and also says, 'Bad puppy.' Which of the two children has knowledge of what really happened? Most likely, the second child. To confirm her suspicion, the mother further interrogates the second child.

Now, you know all this. But there are still many things to know about the connection between surprise and knowledge. These things are the targets of my research.

In my research I ask three questions: one, how did the surprise and expectation connection come about in the first place; that is, how did it evolve over evolutionary time? Two, how does knowledge and its corresponding belief develop in a person's early life? And, three, does surprise suggest how much a child knows, and his or her level of mental development?

I would like to give you definitive answers to these questions, but at present, I cannot. I can, though, give you partial answers based on several studies, but to go into their methodologies would take too much time. As you know, a logical, exact, and transparent methodology is what distinguishes science from many other intellectual exercises. Without good methodology spelled out in great detail for all to see, science is not possible (now to wake them up). I have no time for that here. Perhaps in ten years I will have such answers. So I hope you will invite me back at that time."

Some in the audience laughed, others did not. The chancellor smiled weakly. (he invited the wrong guy)

"Now for questions and discussion."

Silence.

"We still have a bit of time for discussion."

Again, silence. (either they did not understand me, or found it all to obvious, or they are afraid to talk, or just puzzled . . . nevertheless, I will at least get my 'modest honorarium')

"Professor," a saving voice came from a student in the front row. "Do you have any tentative findings to share with us without having to go into so much detail? We will believe your methods are sound."

"Good question. Yes. Using a magic trick, I have observed infants under one year of age—about 10 months. I wanted to determine if they would act surprised when an object they put under a cup disappeared. Its disappearance would surprise a normal adult because it appears as a violation of the concept of conservation of matter. This is a basic physical truth. If infants, too, are surprised, I conclude they already grasp the concept of conservation of matter at that early age. And I found that many of them do and most infants at an earlier age do not. I should mention that a famous child psychologist previously discovered this, but I am a skeptic

and wanted to make sure he was right. Also, I have some age-related findings on the child's understanding of spatial rotation on the linear order
of objects."

"That is very interesting."

"Thank you."

Richard then pointed to an exhausted but eager-looking woman in
the third row who raised her hand (she looks mischievous).

"Was there anything that surprised you when you came to our city?"
She smiled. (be careful . . . no . . . tell her the truth)

"What surprised me was the presence of many tanks and soldiers
outside the train station when I arrived here."

Silence.

She continued smiling. "But you must have already known they were
in the area. You must have read the papers or listened to the radio or seen
it on television."

Richard smiled broadly. "I have and I did know it, but I was still
somewhat surprised—actually, I was a bit scared as well."

"So your theory is not perfect yet?"

"That is correct. I am too young to have a perfect theory."

The audience laughed.

During this interaction, the chancellor sat immobile, then suddenly
stood up. "This has been a very stimulating talk. Now we must adjourn.
Thank you for coming, Professor Richard. And I thank all of you for taking time from your busy schedules to be here tonight." (do they have to be
busy even after 7 P.M.?)

The chancellor and Richard left the lecture hall and walked to a
nearby street where a large luxury car awaited. "We will go to my place
for dinner. My wife is expecting us."

"That would be very nice."

"First, though, I must tank up."

When they arrived at the gas station there was a long line of cars.
"Wait here." The chancellor jumped out of the car with vigor and walked
straight to the station office. Richard could see him talking to an attendant
who nodded several times. The chancellor returned, backed up slightly,
then drove around the car in front of him. He drove to the pump that was
just vacated and the attendant rushed over and began filling his gas tank.
"I know these people and informed them I had an important visitor from
the United States." He looked at Richard and smiled.

"Yes, I understand." (must I be grateful to be seen with an important person . . . and I am grateful I am that person)

At the chancellor's house, his wife greeted them at the door. She was a tall, well-dressed woman, considerably younger than the chancellor. "Please come in, professor, we are delighted you could come."

After an aperitif in silence they went into the dining room (what is this guy thinking?). His son, a young man in his late teens or early twenties, greeted Richard with a very weak handshake and sat down. He said nothing during the meal, but he did drink fully of the wine. (I wonder what he is like and what he thinks of all this)

The hostess was quiet and a bit stiff. (too deferential to authority . . . I ought to try lightening her up a bit . . . but how?)

The conversation had a boring start—mostly about the weather and an art exhibit that Richard must definitely see. Then the topic changed. The son, looking a bit tipsy, suddenly broke in. "What do you think about our new government?" His mother was horrified.

"I do not think much of it. I mean, I have not thought about it much because I simply do not have enough knowledge about your country. Actually, it is one reason I'm glad to be here. I like to know more about your life here since you have a new government." (enough . . . let Mr. Chancellor take over)

"Yes," the chancellor said to Richard. "You cannot have much knowledge of our country because you have seen virtually none of it. But what you have seen so far, you must conclude, is hardly negative. You see our people, our streets, some of academics at our university. We are fundamentally solid, hardworking, and friendly. My guess is we are no different from your own people, other than the recent conflict with our neighbors. This is usually the case when countries are clustered closely together and have different cultures and languages. We have many more close neighbors than the U.S., which in general creates more problems." (he is getting close)

His son broke in. "And, as you know, we are now adjusting to being an invaded country."

"Son, you do not have it right," The chancellor said grimly. "They are not invaders; they are our allies and always have been. They came to save us from some of our own people who have become corrupt and, if I may say so, despicable."

The hostess became increasingly distraught.

The chancellor glared at her as if to say, 'don't dispute me.' "We called our allies in to help us." He paused with a false smile. "Let us have a good brandy now."

He went to a cabinet and brought out a half-full decanter and two brandy snifters.

"Who is 'we'?" Richard tried to act naive. (uh oh . . . going too far)

"Our people—the vast majority of our people," The chancellor said as he poured the brandy. (too much . . . too much . . . his wife must be thinking)

Mrs. Chancellor suddenly got up. "Excuse me. I forgot the dessert." She left the room and a few seconds later called to her husband asking him to help. He slowly got up.

The son took his father's brandy snifter, smiled, and took a big gulp, then a second. (uh oh . . . this is going to be an interesting evening)

The chancellor returned. "You see, democracy must have a start but even before that start it must have sufficient power to ensure stability and law so that people will feel secure and be able to exercise democracy. In the 18th Century, your country had to first fight the lawless and drive out those who did not want democracy. Not until your founding fathers and their successors got control over their enemies was it possible to make democracy a reality for all your people."

"That is correct!" the son burst out triumphantly.

"Actually, it is only partially correct. It was not only the British you Americans drove out, but also the natives that lived in your country before you settled it. Is that not correct, professor?"

"Good. So my father is right."

Richard smiled weakly. "Yes, but since then the world has become more humane and intelligent about having good government. Everyone now knows that all citizens in a democratic country should have a chance to participate in the governance of the country and live free of unjust persecution. We ensure this with an election process."

"Ha, but only after you drove your enemies out of your country," the chancellor responded.

The hostess interrupted. "Yes, I think we are all clear on this, so let us enjoy the dessert."

"No," the chancellor said, revealing his anger. "I think Professor Richard is insinuating that our country is not justified in defending itself from its internal enemies and will not allow democracy to take root here.

Well, we are justified in dealing with them, but unlike your country we do not drive them out. We allow them to stay here and treat them as well as everyone else—as long as they do not engage in anti-government activities. So far we have done nothing to them. We have not even put the well-known guilty on trial. We are a humane people who follow laws." (he is out of control . . . time to get out of here)

Richard looked at him directly (don't appear intimidated). "I am glad to hear that. I take your word for it. I just ask questions because I have no full knowledge of what goes on here. When anyone goes to a country as a visitor they do not know what goes on behind its walls. Therefore, anyone who has not crossed the borders or gone behind the walls cannot claim to be an expert on that country. I am clearly one of them." (now, now . . . don't sound too appeasing . . . he won't believe you . . . or he will and then try to push you around)

"Huh," the chancellor waved his hand in disgust and struck his brandy snifter, sending it to the floor. He stared at the broken glass and got up. "Excuse me," he said, and left the room unsteadily.

His wife turned to Richard. "He has had a long day and there are very many pressures on him. I am sure you understand."

"I do, and now I must get back to where I am staying."

"I am afraid you must walk," she said apologetically. "Anyone driving with too much alcohol in his blood must pay a very large fine. And the police look for such people at this time of night."

"I understand. I will walk. Thank you very much for your kind dinner invitation."

"Our son will show you how to get home. Good night and thank you for visiting us."

The cool night air out on the street was refreshing. Richard looked at the young man a bit skeptically. "Okay, which way do I go?"

"It is not difficult, if you listen carefully to me." The son smiled sarcastically (jerk). "Go to the end of this street and turn left at the first street. You got that? "

Richard nodded.

"You are staying down by the river near our famous bridge. Is that correct?"

Richard nodded.

"Okay. As you know, water flows downhill, eventually to rivers which flow to the sea. Soooo, if you keep going downhill you will get to the river.

Understand? (bigger jerk). Now the river flows to the right when you get to it. If you look, you will see that it flows to the right and when it does it will flow under our famous bridge. Do you understand all this?"

"I think so. Straight ahead to the first left, turn left, go and go and go downhill to the river, then make a sharp right, a very sharp right. Is that right, really right? (don't wait for an answer) I suspect the water is cold and wet so I should not walk into it."

"Right! You know very much."

"Then make a sharp right and go to the bridge and from there it is all very easy."

"Sir, there is no question: you are a very intelligent person." (and there is no question you are a bigger jerk than any intelligent person I know)

Richard headed down the street and noticed how dark everything was. The new government had no time, or desire, to turn on the streetlights. At least there was the moon, but it was only partially helpful; clouds were continuously moving across it. House windows were shuttered. The whole town looked like it was in a blackout. (maybe the government keeps the lights off to save energy . . . or to keep people in their houses)

Stumbling over curbs, bumping into unknown stationary objects, hitting tree and shrub branches with his arms, Richard reached a flat area that appeared to be a park. He saw a couple on a bench hugging each other and murmuring, then heard someone strumming a guitar in the dark—it was the song "Mrs. Robinson." (well . . . civilization exists even here . . . God bless you Mr. Guitarist . . . Jesus loves you more)

Across a broad street paralleled by a promenade, the river appeared, black and ominous. He turned right on a street lined with large sycamore trees. Next to them stretched spacious sidewalks flanked by large gray-stone buildings. (government buildings no doubt . . . big, faceless authorities)

The darkness amplified the silence. He felt peace for the first time since he arrived in the city. The moon, the dear moon, emerged from behind he clouds.

Crash! In front of him and to the side a giant bronze door opened and a large black car roared out and onto the street. The giant door slammed shut behind it. The car raced about fifty yards and then slowed down. The rear door on the right swung open and a form tumbled out onto the street. The door slammed shut and the car zoomed off.

Richard stood there, stunned (what in the world is that?), then ran toward the form crumpled on the street. (now what . . . what to do . . . tricky . . . don't get involved . . . but the guy must be hurting)

He stopped and leaned over him. Just then, he heard a door in the same building open. A huge figure emerged. It was a man in a black coat. He came toward Richard with long strides (time to leave). Richard straightened up and ran off. (too big to handle . . . stay out of it . . . can't win this one)

The giant stared at Richard, then gave the man in the street a kick and walked back to the building. After walking two blocks, Richard came to Auntie's apartment (safe at home). The outside door was locked. There was a bell next to it and he pushed it three, four, five times. He could hear the bell ringing in the lobby, but there was no response. (now what?)

He crossed the street to get a view of Auntie's windows. No light was seen. (she's fast asleep . . . also without her hearing aid . . . wonder whether it works)

He stood and waited a few seconds (okay, time to take a nap). He sat down with his back to the apartment wall and pulled his jacket up over his ears.

Richard heard footsteps. A woman hurried on the other side of the street. She fished her keys out of her purse and began opening the apartment door.

"Wait." Richard jumped up. She looked at Richard, quickly opened the door, and disappeared.

Richard ran across the street and began ringing the bell. No response. He went back across the street to keep an eye on Auntie's windows. (she's still fast asleep)

The heat he built up on his trip down to the river began dissipating (now the cold part). A door in the apartment opened and a man appeared. "I could hear you ringing the bell over there. I know you are a guest there. She is sleeping and even if you could get into the lobby, she could not hear you ringing. Come in here. You will catch a cold out here. Yes, I know you are her American visitor. She told me you were coming and I have seen you several times come out of there."

"Thank you, thank you so much."

"You can stay in our place. It is small. You can sleep on our sofa. I have a pillow and blanket for you."

"You are very kind."

"Please make no noise. My wife is a light sleeper."

Richard entered his apartment. It must have been furnished in the 1930s.

"Good night, sir." (he is kind and shy)

"Good night. I appreciate your kindness."

His host went into the bedroom and locked the door.

Richard awoke at about 7 A.M. His host heard him and appeared at his bedroom door.

"I will go now," Richard said. "Thank you very much. You are very kind."

"Do not mention it. I would offer you some coffee but we are a bit short now."

"I understand. Again thank you." Richard shook his hand and left.

He and Auntie had a lively conversation. She was interested in his lecture and especially the chancellor. "You should know," she said a bit conspiratorially, "he is in a new position made especially for him by our new rulers. He does not have a good past. One must be very careful around him. He is very ambitious."

"I gathered that." Richard decided not to mention the episode on the street in front of the government building. He then began packing his things to leave. He looked out the window onto a side street. His rental car was still there and as far as he could see, still had two rear wheels and hubcaps. (I'm really getting paranoid)

"Oh, yes, before I go," Richard pulled some bills out of his wallet. "Here is a little something for your wonderful hospitality."

"No, no. That is not necessary."

"It would make your niece very happy if you accepted it. Actually, most of it is hers (white lies are allowed now and then). Also, this is for the very nice man across the street who gave me a bed for the night." He laid a few bills on the table.

"Oh, yes, he is a very nice man. He also is not popular with the new government, so we are good friends—secretly, of course. Now, I have only one more request for you; Actually, two. First, have a safe trip."

"Of course."

"And this," She held up a large eider down pillow. "Could you please take this with you? It belongs to my niece. She has had it since she was a little girl, and she still feels it's one of her best friends."

"Oh! I would like to take it, but you remember what happened last time. Those border officials kept everything but my backpack."

"I understand, but if we don't try, we will have no success in beating them. Besides, you can always tell them it is yours. How would they know? And if they don't believe it, then what? What would they do with it? Take it home?"

"Okay, boss." After a big hug and several poorly suppressed tears, they parted.

Richard went down to the car and loaded his backpack and the pillow. Suddenly the chancellor's son appeared.

"Hey, hey, professor!" He held an envelope in his hand. "My father says this is for you. Your honorarium, I guess."

"Thank you very much and thank him as well." Richard slipped the envelope into his jacket pocket.

"So you followed my directions and got back here safely."

(should I tell him . . . ? I will . . . to see if he has a strong surprise reaction) "I did, but not too far from here in front of one of your impressive government buildings there was an incident."

"Oh!" (a bit of surprise . . . he may suspect something bad)

"Yes, it was unpleasant." Richard watched his face closely. "A black limousine came out of one of the buildings and dumped a man onto the street. I went to help him, but a big man, a very big man, in black came up to me so I ran off—like a coward. And then the big man kicked the man lying in the street."

"Yes, and what should I do about it?" (he blanched a bit . . . now he's blushing)

"Tell your father, of course. He should know this, especially in light of our conversation last evening."

The young man flushed. "He drank too much. He has had a very hard life until . . . until. You are getting judgmental again. Maybe you should be reminded what happened to your Indians?" (now he is really mad)

The young man walked away. (acquiring unpleasant knowledge is usually painful)

4

DIFFICULT DEPARTURE

Richard took a new road to the border (shouldn't get to be too well-known around here). As the road approached the border, it turned into the familiar zigzag path before it was blocked by a large iron pipe on hinges. A guard approached, took a quick look inside his car, and pushed the pipe away. Richard drove slowly and stopped. (today I am a very good boy)

"Good morning," an official in a green uniform saluted. "Have you had a good visit to our country?"

"Magnificent."

"Passport please." He looked at it. "Is this your vehicle?"

"Yes, but it is a rental vehicle."

"I see. May I have the rental papers?"

"Yes."

He studied them carefully, walked to the front of the car, looked at the license plate, and wrote it down. Another official appeared on the scene. "Now, sir, would you bring your bag there and come inside?"

"Certainly." (now what is his problem?) Richard followed them and placed his backpack on the counter.

"Would you open it please?" The official went through it. He saw Richard's tie, the green-striped one he wore at his talk. He ran his thumb and index finger down it in a pinching movement (looking for what? a folded letter?). "Could I see how much money you are carrying?"

"Certainly." Richard opened his wallet and pulled out his bills. (interesting that he has not asked for the contents of my jacket pocket . . . maybe this time)

"I assume you changed this at our border when you entered." The official held up a bunch of bills.

"Of course. Here is the exchange receipt."

The official looked at it closely. "You did not spend much on your stay in our city."

"No, I was fortunate to be able to stay at a colleague's apartment. (better move off that topic quickly). Oh, yes—that is not all the money I have." Richard took his honorarium envelope out of his jacket pocket and opened it. (wow . . . about eight American dollars worth)

"What is that?"

"I was given this by your university for a talk I gave there."

"Hmm. Well, you must turn in all your money here."

"What do you mean by that?"

"We are not a bank. We have no foreign currency here."

"What! You can't mean I lose my money, the money given to me by your government? What kind of government do you have here? (now, now Richard, take it easy . . . you are still in their trap)

Ignoring the question, the official looked at Richard. "You can spend this money in our store here," he pointed to another room. "There are many nice souvenirs you can buy there to remember our new country. You can leave your bag here. It will be safe." He turned and went out the front door.

Richard went into the store (kitsch . . . some dry cookies . . . bottles of schnaps . . . lots of schnaps). He left the store with lots of schnaps—enough to last many months.

Outside, he had to catch his breath. Three officials were looking through his car. The back seat was pulled out and lying on the ground. The trunk was open and an official was walking around with a mirror fastened to the end of a stick to see under the car.

"What are you doing?" Richard asked. "Is this how you treat a visitor to your university? Where is a telephone?"

"Sir, this is routine procedure." The official motioned to one of his colleagues, who put the seat back in the car and closed the trunk.

Richard put his backpack on the back seat, turned around, and got a rude shock. One of the officials was holding the pillow Auntie gave him.

Richard glared at him. "What are you doing with that?"

The other official quickly came over to Richard, "We want to know where you got this pillow."

"You must be kidding me. That is my pillow."

"Sir." A big smile broke over the official's face. The other two officials were smirking (jerks). "This is not your pillow."

"It is. I always take it with me when I travel."

"Excuse me, sir, but we know for sure this is not your pillow and all we want to know whose pillow this is. When you tell us, you can go."

(b. . . st . . . rds)." It is my pillow."

"We are sorry to tell you this, but it is not your pillow because when you crossed our border—not here, but north of here—this pillow was not in your car."

"Your country is surely a great country when you pay important border officials to be interested in people's pillows. (they may want Auntie's name and address and then can trace her niece)

"Just the name of the person and then you can go."

Richard looked across the border to the other side. The official in the adjacent country was watching this exchange with binoculars. (ah freedom . . . there is freedom . . . there is democracy . . . but I am not telling them Auntie's name)

"Gentlemen," he looked at the three of them one by one, slowly and without expression. "This is my pillow."

Two of the subordinate officials looked warily a their boss. He hesitated a moment and looked expressionlessly at Richard. "You may go."

"Thank you." Richard took the pillow from his hand and threw it into the car.

The officials turned around. One signaled the guard at the other barrier. The guard opened the barrier and saluted Richard as he slowly drove by. Richard returned the salute with a big smile (you b . . . st . . . rds . . . and god bless America!). He hoped the guard did not understand him.

5

COMPETING FOR RESOURCES

RICHARD'S EXPERIENCES IN THE invaded country revived memories of his early intelligence work, mostly of malevolent authorities harassing and persecuting the weak and vulnerable. For him the crucial question persisted: how do these authorities become that way? Weren't they once innocent children—perhaps with a bit of a mean streak in some of them? Bullying occurs everywhere, but usually diminishes with age, so why do some adults engage in heartless violence against others? Is adult violence a reflection of an innate tendency possessed by a certain percentage of every population in every culture, no matter what life circumstances are involved?

Experts in child development already had convincing evidence for two general factors responsible for cultivating future tendencies toward violence: neglect and abuse during childhood. Both were capable of damaging early social relationships, which in turn culminated in destructive and criminal behavior later in life. These two factors could also culminate in depression and suicide.

Richard pushed the issue deeper by exploring the main purpose of social relationships. In his many observations of young children in nursery schools and kindergartens, Richard noticed their social relationships revolved around getting what they wanted—a toy, a place in line for a treat, a playmate, a parent's affection, or teacher's attention. In other words, he observed that children engaged in social interactions to acquire something. This something he labeled "resources"—things every child (and, of course, every adult) needed in his or her daily life.

It was at this point in his studies that Richard grasped the importance of economics in everyday life. Every human depends on outside resources to survive, to be comfortable and happy. These resources include such obvious things as food, shelter, clothing, comfort, safety, affection, recognition by society, and sources of novelty.

The problem of such dependency was that resources were very seldom in ample supply, and competition was inevitable. He witnessed these tensions among adults in the invaded country. Its citizens lost control over resources to a foreign power. For young children, competition was usually not fierce and prolonged, especially if they had kind parents with adequate material means. Competition occurred, of course, with siblings and peers, but usually not for long. Later in life, though, competition could escalate and in some circumstances become deadly. Resource competition was a bio-economic fact to which all living organisms are heir.

Richard soon came to believe that a major part of growing up involved learning how to compete for resources. Fierce fighting was not the only option; other strategies were also available: cooperation and reciprocity, or less positive strategies like deception, manipulation, and intimidation. The important task for each child was learning how and when to apply and balance these various strategies—depending on the circumstances at the time.

Richard realized that since his hypothesis was dealing with a general fact of life he had to prove that learning how to balance such strategies was a universal problem for children. This meant he had to study children first-hand in various cultures if he wanted to observe how and when this learning took place. Since he liked traveling and working with children, this would be an ideal way to spend his research time—for what he hoped would be years to come.

Before I report on his first research trip focusing on children in a distant country, allow me turn you over to William.

"William here: before I met Richard, as I already mentioned, I served in military intelligence. When I was discharged, I kept in contact with colleagues, as many veterans do. When my colleagues discovered where I was teaching they informed me that Richard was at the same university. They thought I might like to get to know him, but they also hinted that I should keep an eye on his activities. Like me, he had had top-secret clearance, which meant he still possessed sensitive information about intelligence activities.

As you know, disgruntled employees can turn against their employers. Richard was never disgruntled as far as I know, though he did mention being upset by certain tactics his intelligence unit once used to get vital information from an individual considered an enemy.

You must understand; in intelligence work nothing is sacred except secrecy and loyalty to one's country. This means that even one's colleagues in intelligence are not—should not be—sacred. In the regular army, buddies are always sacred, but not in intelligence. Yes, this sounds terrible, but it is absolutely necessary. Security is vital to national survival; without it there are no freedom or democracy. Loyalty to colleagues that jeopardize this security is criminal. All this is pretty black and white when you get down to it. Yes, I know, you may find this state of affairs appalling, but that's the way the world works. As for Richard, he does not know about my obligations to keep a fatherly eye on him.

I mention all this now because Richard just received a grant to conduct research on children in a distant country, a country that has some serious problems with U.S. foreign policy. For this reason, I have misgivings about him going there. Anyway, let us get back to his planned trip."

Richard was in his office the day before his trip when William stopped by to chat. He and Richard had already disagreed on the risks of traveling to unfriendly places. "Once again," William warned, "unexpected things can happen on travels, especially to those countries not fond of the U.S."

"Yes, I know, but you exaggerate these things. And if they do happen, I think I can handle them."

"Quite confident, aren't you? Many unforeseeable things can happen that put any traveler at risk—kidnapping, for example. Just being in the wrong place at the wrong time. Happens all the time."

"I know, but . . . "

Richard's secretary suddenly appeared at the door. "A gentleman to see you."

A tall man about 35 years of age wearing a dark-blue suit and a red-and-white striped tie entered the room. "Good morning. I work for U.S. Security." He showed them his ID and shook hands with both men. (Afterward, Richard and William called him 'Mr. Security.')

"I heard that you, Professor Richard, are going to Country X."

"Yes." Richard smiled.

"As you know, Country X currently has a mixed reaction to our foreign policy. Our relations with them are becoming less friendly by the hour, it seems. Your safety may be jeopardized."

"And?"

"And, as is standard operation procedure with countries that could become, shall we say, problematic, we try to collect as much up-to-date information about them as possible. The reasons for this are obvious."

"I see. That means you want . . . "

"Yes, your help. It's simple. When tourists go to exotic places, they usually take photos or video records of what they see. You do use a video camera in your research, don't you?"

"Yes." (now how did he know that . . . and what about my safety . . . it'll be interesting how William reacts to this)

"Well, our agency would appreciate it if you also shot scenes that may be important for us in the future—building projects, road widening, bunkers, construction sites for possible air fields, new hydroelectric plants—general indicators of possible military and related economic usage. As you know, up-to-date video shots of such sites can be extremely valuable."

"I know what you mean," Richard said.

"Would you consent to do that?"

William watched this scene with great interest.

Richard hesitated. "O.K. I'll do my best." (why not . . . no harm . . . intelligence gathering is always a good substitute for fighting a war . . . but . . .)

"Good. By the way, you must know I'm aware that you have an intelligence background."

"I figured you did."

"So you understand the absolute need for secrecy."

"I do. And William, here, I'm sure does as well." Richard looked at William.

"I do." William answered.

"And suppose I raise suspicions in Country X, what then?"

"You're on your own on this one."

(ouch . . . William, did you hear that?) "I understand."

"Do you have enough videotapes?"

"I do."

"Then have a safe trip. Goodbye, gentlemen." Mr. Security got up, shook hands, and walked out.

"Whew! And on it goes—the struggle for power never stops," Richard sighed.

"Right. Have a safe trip, old friend." William looked serious.

"I will."

The next day on the plane, Richard became unusually restless. The flight meal was okay, and the glass of chardonnay soothing, but two potential problems had already ruined his mood: the difficulty of doing good scientific research under less-than-ideal circumstances, and the immediate issue (ten hours to go) of getting into a country with his project and equipment. There was always the possibility that some official would simply refuse him entry on any pretext, like the traveler is too inquisitive about the country or seems like a troublemaker. Richard knew he had to tread carefully. As for taking the video shots for Mr. Security, Richard temporarily forgot about it. His research plan occupied all this thoughts.

In addition to doing research and traveling, Richard had an ultimate goal: to help children by teaching them to become more cooperative and to share with others. He believed that teaching them about fairness and justice would in the future make the ground less fertile for the seeds of war.

His immediate plan was to provide kids with a competition task while he recorded their behavior for the permanent record. In addition to observing them in this contrived situation—the competition task—he would observe their everyday behaviors and environments as much as possible.

The competition task was quite simple: Richard presented four children (picked at random from a classroom) with a device called the Fun-Cartoon Machine. If they wanted to see the cartoon (located on a video cartridge inserted into the machine) they would have to cooperate with each other. By cooperating, each child could get to see the cartoon—perhaps not as long as an individual child may want, but long enough. This was the invariable price of sharing—get something, not everything. The price of not sharing, of simply fighting or refusing to cooperate, was clear—one person would get much viewing time at the expense of others, or no one would get any viewing time. Invariably the outcome would be bad. Social inequity never leads to peace and permanent satisfaction.

Since the game is a standard situation it can be used all over the world to compare and analyze children's behavior, and to connect them to such variables as culture, social class, age, and gender. However, the whole study would be for naught unless he got the Fun-Cartoon Machine past the border officials. Many officials at border checkpoints hope for someone unusual to come to their desk—a chance to break up the monotony or just exercise their authority. Richard's reasons for being there were unusual, as was his Fun-Cartoon Machine.

While Richard was mulling over how to cross the border with the least amount of trouble, his plane landed. It was dawn and all he saw at first were a few lights in the distance. Then the landscape slowly appeared—soft, smoky hills, mostly barren but beautiful in the emerging sunlight.

The airport terminal sharply contrasted the serenity of the landscape—bright lights, smells of over-ripe lunches, sporadic shouts, exhausted travelers, some with nervous smiles, others cool and businesslike. Richard felt his throat get dry and his stomach muscles tighten.

At the customs desk, a female official in baggy brown trousers and a faded shirt with red shoulder insignias slowly rolled up her sleeves. She studied Richard for a moment, then asked for his passport. "Why are you visiting our country?"

"I'm a scientist studying children all over the world."

"Why?"

"I want to understand them, to know what they do, in school and as they grow up."

"What do you plan to do with the children?"

"Let them play with this machine." Richard lifted it in front of her. "I call it a Fun-Cartoon Machine. Children like to see the cartoons when they look through here." He pointed to the viewing piece. "I videotape them with my camcorder." He held it up to her.

She was not impressed. "Who do you represent?"

"Our university. It's in the Midwest of the United States. I'm a professor there. Here is a letter from our university research director."

She glanced at the letterhead, turned, and motioned to a second official.

The second official picked up the machine. Richard suddenly blurted out, "When you look in here, you can see a cartoon. Wanna see it?" (stupid thing to say)

The official ignored the request, turned the machine around, then asked to see Richard's camcorder. Richard handed it to him. He looked at it, handed it back, and rummaged through Richard's travel bag. The first official wrote in a notebook. "You can go."

Richard weakly thanked her, picked up his stuff, and headed for the taxi stand.

He took a nap in the hotel, showered, changed his money, and took another cab to the school. He was happy. (it's great to work with kids . . . no matter where . . . they are the hope of the world . . . I'd like to take them all back with me for a canoe trip up north . . . fun and good for them to learn to get along)

The school at the edge of the city was a dilapidated three-story build-ing with gray-brown stucco walls and a roof of cracked clay shingles—a sad-looking, neglected place for children. Inside, the children were recit-ing, singing, and occasionally laughing.

The teachers he met in the halls were generally friendly but appeared washed out and sluggish. The school principal was livelier, better dressed, and seemed impressed by her own authority. She watched Richard casu-ally as he pulled out his wallet and handed her money. "This is for your school library as a gift from America," he explained. She accepted the bills with a faint grin. "Yes, of course, for the library." (I bet)

"Now I must introduce you to our head teacher.

The head teacher, a tall, solemn woman, greeted him pleasantly and gave Richard a tour of the school. Then she stopped at a classroom. "This is the classroom you will start with. They are second graders."

She opened the classroom door. Fifty faces looked up at him. (here they are, the future . . . who will be cooperative . . . who will make trouble . . . this will be very interesting)

"Hello. I am going to see you tomorrow to show you how to play a game." He smiled broadly.

No response.

"Say hello to our guest from America." The head teacher raised her finger and smiled.

"Hello!" (not overwhelming . . . it's good that they are careful with strangers)

The next day he set his Fun-Cartoon Machine in the front of the classroom and his camcorder at a distance in a corner. (good I brought batteries . . . no electric outlet here)

He picked four children to play the game. They had to figure out how to work the machine so they could see the cartoon. They learned im-mediately what had to be done—one took over the viewing piece, another released the brake on the crank, and the third turned the crank and the cartoon went into action. The fourth child stood and waited. Each group was given ten minutes.

Some groups took turns and shared viewing time; some were domi-
nated by one or two children; some struggled and argued and thereby lost
much or all of their viewing time. One group had a clown who entertained
the others with fabulous stories about what he saw in the viewing piece.
He took up the whole time allotted to his group, joking all the while.
(great distraction strategy . . . fooled the others into working for him . .
an interesting but not totally uncommon strategy)

At the end of the morning, Richard felt good. The children found the
game a lot of fun. For him their behavior was theoretically very important—they acted like American children despite the cultural differences
between them. Richard's search for universal behaviors and strategies
seemed to be paying off. The head teacher was pleased; it seemed Richard's
visit was a good distraction for everyone.

He stayed at the school for a week; much of his time was spent waiting to get into a classroom. By the end of the week, he was getting at-
tached to the children and some of the school staff. The head teacher was
enthusiastic about the project and very interesting to talk to.

His next destination was another school farther out in the country.
The bus ride was bumpy and crowded, but he enjoyed it immensely. The
landscape got more rugged with ridges and valleys crisscrossed with un-
paved roads running next to scattered mud-and-stone huts. Snow-capped
mountains rose above a layer of dusty air that hovered over the sparse
grassland.

The locals appeared to be mostly farmers or herders. Richard found
it impossible to figure out what they were feeling or thinking. They were
polite but kept their distance, aware that Richard was watching them.

Two weeks later, Richard was exhausted. He forgot how many groups
he videotaped—over forty, which was a good sample for comparison with
other countries. He also shot footage of several sites for Mr. Security. He
sandwiched video clips of the sites between clips of school children and
mixed them with standard tourist shots (more difficult to find that way).
He began to feel successful.

The time came for the long journey back to the hotel in the city. As
he was getting on bus, he instantly sensed great excitement; something
big had happened somewhere. Then it slowly came out—a horrific catastrophe back in the U.S.—airplanes crashed into and destroyed buildings.
Many people were killed.

Back at the hotel he watched the scenes of destruction on television: a devastating surprise attack on the U.S. with a terrible loss of life! The reaction in the hotel verged on chaos. In the lobby the hotel personnel avoided looking at him. His only thought was to get home fast. He gathered his backpack and equipment and immediately arranged for a taxi to the airport. He refused to pay his hotel bill until the taxi arrived. He no longer trusted anyone. He grabbed his things in the lobby and left without saying goodbye to the staff. If he had, nobody would have heard him.

Armed men were standing around the airport waiting room. Several of them looked closely at Richard and his Fun-Cartoon Machine. Richard noticed and gestured to them. "Hi, this is for kids! Cartoons for kids."

They looked at him curiously (actually, that was a weird thing to say to them). Richard turned away, pulled a book out of his jacket, and started reading. (people calmly reading books are not dangerous . . . oops . . . here's Charlie Check-point)

"Hi!" Richard handed the official his passport.

The official looked at it. "Why did you visit our country?"

"'I am a scientist and I study children all over the world. I like children and want to understand them. I let them watch cartoons with this." He held up his machine.

The official looked at it briefly. "What's in there?" He pointed to Richard's plastic bag full of videotapes.

"Videotapes of school children. Science. I am a scientist".

The official motioned to his colleague; they spoke in hushed voices then one called Richard over to him. "Come. Bring everything." (here we go) Richard picked up his stuff and followed him.

The official led Richard into a room with several chairs, a couple of shelves, and a wooden desk. "Please sit down." A man behind the desk pointed to a chair.

Richard tried to remember his rules while being on the hot seat: (a) be honest about everything (well, almost everything; white lies are occasionally allowed for 'ethical' purposes); (b) tell officials that you work with children all over the world; (c) give no names of places you visited (your excuse, if asked, being that you do not know their language); (d) insist you travel to many other countries to study children, the results of which will be published in a scientific report; (e) always be respectful (even your worst enemy will not object to be being treated respectfully); and (f) never show any sign of weakness by smiling too much.

After following these rules—more or less—Richard was not sure if the officials understood or believed him. Then the first official muttered something to the guard, who left and returned with a modestly dressed civilian wearing steel-rimmed glasses and a short, clean beard. Compared to the others, he looked more urbane and distinguished.

He looked Richard in the eye. "Hello, I am the district minister of culture. I hear you are interested in studying our children."

"Yes, I am, along with children from many other countries as well. I have a hypothesis that everyone in the world has to learn to cooperate with others in order to survive. The problem is faced by many higher species (uh oh, I'm going into too much depth . . . but he still seems interested). Humans are no different; they need resources to survive and since all humans need roughly the same resources, they will, sooner or later, have to compete for them. And, as I am sure you know, there are various ways to do that—like fighting, cheating, or cooperating with them and sharing the resources. (pause a bit so he gets it)

Richard continued. "I think people in general learn these ways when they are children. So it is important we know how they learn, and under what circumstances, so we can cultivate better ways for them to use productive strategies. So they can get along with others—cooperatively and peacefully. Otherwise, we'll always have war."

The district minister of culture stared at Richard with cautious interest. "That's quite a jump you make. Yes, I understand. Our scholars and even our average citizens are familiar with this problem, actually for centuries, and have come to a similar conclusion as you. Peace can only come about through cooperation. So why do you still go to the trouble of doing all this research?"

"Because I am skeptical about many things people claim are true—including scholars if they cannot back their claims with scientific facts. Knowledge must be based on facts, not opinions. Scientists collect facts, analyze them, and report their results to others. That's my job".

"And videotaping children will provide you with these facts?"

"Yes, of course. Videotape records are permanent and can be looked at repeatedly by different scientists. Of course, they give us only a small part of the bigger picture. As you know, great monuments are constructed with thousands of little stones. What I'm doing here is gathering some of these stones."

"I agree, but stories can also deal with facts, and stories can make facts more interesting. All a storyteller needs is good observation skills and memory, some imagination, and the right words—not fancy machines and videotapes. As you surely know, for thousands of years before science, storytelling has been a universal way to teach people all the important things they need to know."

"That's what my friend William says."

"What do you think you will conclude from your videotapes?"

"That some children know how to be bold and bully the weaker; others will be shy and withdrawn. Some will be left out and disappointed, others will cooperate and share. Only a few will get to enjoy life fully because they have access to many resources. A majority will grow up disappointed because they fail to get what they want. Growing up with disappointment can easily lead to frustration and anger, which can easily lead to violence."

"Of course, but that is hardly new."

"Also, I think I will be able to conclude that children act pretty much the same all over the world. This suggests that what they learn may well be universal—perhaps a biological universal. More importantly, what I have observed so far is that groups that cooperate usually end up getting more resources overall than groups that fight. Fighting usually destroys resources. If kids all over the world can learn this they are more likely to cooperate with other as adults. This could mean the end of war and a better world in general."

"Ah, you Americans are always naive and optimistic"

"Better than always pessimistic."

"Perhaps. But now I must be honest with you. Being from that part of the world that is currently pessimistic, I must tell you that it is my duty to look carefully at what you have on your videotapes."

"But my plane leaves in a few minutes."

"You won't miss your flight, but you must leave your tapes here with us. After I examine them, I will send them to you. As for your machine, we will take a photo of it." A guard quickly snapped a photo of the device. "Your machine does not appear dangerous; you can take it home with you and continue your research there." He smiled. "Thank your for your time. It has been interesting to hear about your work." While leaving, he motioned to the guard to give Richard his Fun-Cartoon Machine and his backpack, which had been thoroughly searched during the interrogation.

As Richard was about to leave the room, the first official at the desk stopped him. "Do not worry. Your tapes will be sent to you. But to cover the cost, we need funds. It will cost a hundred dollars."

"What! That small bag!" Richard looked around for the minister of culture, but he'd already left. "All I have is 36 dollars."

The official smiled. "That will have to do. As you know, our country is still in an early developmental phase and has some way to go to catch up to the United States. It's always good for countries to cooperate with each other and for the rich ones, especially, to share resources."

So that's how it went with Richard's first research trip. His tapes were gone, but at least he had his Fun-Cartoon Machine. Then something unexpected happened.

As Richard was leaving the room, the minister of culture approached him. "I will see that you get to your plane on time," he said loudly with a smile. And then in a whisper, "In about a month, you will hear from a student who will be coming to your university. I hope you will help this student adjust to university life and to your country."

"Well, I will . . . I will think about . . . I guess."

"Thank you." Then the minister abruptly left.

Richard walked slowly to the gate. (no worries . . . I get that kind of request pretty often when I travel . . . usually nothing happens)

When Richard arrived in the U.S., he immediately called William. "I'm back in one piece. Meet you for coffee."

William got to the cafe first. "Welcome back, my friend. I hear you had a great trip."

"Don't get funny. The experts over there confiscated my tapes and our officials confiscated my Fun-Cartoon Machine."

"Not surprising. Since the catastrophe, security has become our main priority. This country is in serious trouble, Richard. I'm glad you're back."

"Uh oh. Speaking of national security, here comes Mr. Security." (how did he know we were here?)

Looking exhausted, the Mr. Security came over to their table. "Hello. Remember me?" He shook hands with William and Richard. "Professor Richard, I hear you arrived at our airport and our authorities took your equipment. It will be returned to you after they look at it a bit more closely. Do you have the videotapes?"

"No. They took them from me just as I was leaving the country."

"What?" He hesitated a moment. "Did you have anything on the tapes before you left here?"

"I beg your pardon. The tapes were new, still cellophane-wrapped when I left here. I did get some shots of things you told me to look for. They're stuck deep into the tape along with the kids and tourist shots. If those guys just look at the first five or ten minutes of the kids, they most likely will get bored and not look further and return the tapes. I gave them 36 dollars to cover the postage."

" Hmm." He looked at Richard and William and hesitated several seconds. "We'll keep in touch. Good to see you, gentlemen," he said and walked away.

William looked at Richard, "I don't envy him. His job just got tougher in a zillion ways. Our country is really hurting now and we don't want it to continue. As for you, old buddy, your trip was interesting. But you don't have tapes from which you can derive hard facts. However, I have beginning material for a story entitled 'Richard's fruitless travels.' Not bad for this little old writer sitting all the time on the sidelines."

"Funny, funny, but the tapes may still appear."

"Possible, but improbable."

"But I may get an interesting visitor one of these days."

"What do you mean by that?"

Richard told him about the student the minister of culture said may soon be enrolling in the local university

"Ah, ha! Could be interesting. But most likely will not happen."

"But if it does, I can learn something from this student."

"Sure, but no one will know if what the student tells you about his country and its children is at all true. Remember, dear friend, people who live under difficult circumstances often have a real problem with telling the truth unless it serves their survival purposes."

"Yes, I know that, but it would be unfortunate because a local contact could help my research immensely."

"Could be, but all this doesn't matter these days. I'm afraid people don't really think much about the connection between what children learn and future peace. And when they read, they like to read for entertainment—fun stories, not little science stories about how kids learn to make peace."

"Could be, but I still want to persevere so that someday I can teach kids about it."

"Sounds preachy and a bit old-fashion, and, sorry to say, somewhat naive and sanctimonious. Such teaching will never be popular, except maybe to those who already have the message. But I admit, it's better than . . ."

"Killing each other over resources?"

"Precisely."

6

SURPRISE ARRIVAL

"WELL, RICHARD, I'M SURE the memories of your last trip deserve a good story, which you must tell me some time in more detail," William said eagerly. "But I have something interesting to tell you that requires no delay."

"I'm sure, but as not as interesting as my trip." Richard leaned back in the soft chair. (this cafe has class . . . a smoky, conspiratorial atmosphere where undergraduates hammer out their plans to alter the universe)

"Don't be too hasty, my dear friend, to tell me your story." William put both elbows on the table—somewhat jauntily—and rested his chin on his folded hands. "What I have to say requires your careful attention. Just this morning, a letter arrived at our department. It had no return address. It turned out to be from the minister of culture you met in the airport. The student he referred to you is coming to town."

"What? Was the letter addressed to me?"

William pulled the letter from his leather smoking jacket. "As I walked by your mailbox, I saw the letter, but it had no return address and I had the feeling it may be dangerous so I took the liberty of opening it—because we are such good friends and what are good friends for?"

"Of course." (hardly a reason . . . getting a bit nosey, old friend) Richard tried to disguise his anger at this impertinence. "And?"

"Here it is. 'Dear Sir. As I informed you during your departure from our country, I was hoping you would share a gesture of international co-operation, which, I admit, I was sure you would support. As a first step of this cooperation, we have arranged for one of our better students to attend classes at your university. We are hoping that you will host this student who, I have been informed, has the proper authorization papers. This student will contact you on arrival and fill you in on everything. I am confident you will find this satisfactory and hope you will allow us to reciprocate in some form or other in the near future. Respectfully yours, district minister of culture."

William smiled.

"What nerve!" Richard muttered. "I told him I would think about it."

"He is a man of initiative and prompt action, so he must be very competent at what he does." William gave that smile Richard never liked.

"Let's wait and see," Richard said.

A week later, Richard found a note on his desk from his secretary. "Just got a phone call. The student will be at the downtown bus station tomorrow. Bus arriving at 2:15 P.M."

The next day, Richard decided to put on old clothes and carry a small suitcase. He wanted to observe the student first before making contact. He was not sure what to expect and a few precautions never hurt. If he could get an idea of what the student was like before they met, he would be better able to handle the situation.

He and William drove to the bus station but got caught in traffic and did not arrive at the station until about 2:25. No problem; busses never run on time. William waited in his car in the parking lot.

Richard entered the waiting room, took a seat with his back to the wall, and opened a newspaper (just like the good old days in intelligence). The room had six people in it: an elderly man in a wrinkled wind-breaker, two teenage boys, a middle-age woman with a younger woman (possibly her daughter), and an elderly, well-dressed couple who looked out of place. No student.

A few minutes later a group of passengers entered the waiting room and rushed out. No student (I'll wait until 3:10 then check at the desk about the 2:15 bus).

The elderly man and teenage boys suddenly got up and left. Richard went to the desk and learned that the 2:15 had arrived on time (so he didn't make it). He walked to the door and was about to open it, when the young woman, whom Richard assumed was the daughter of the middle-age woman, approached him.

"Sir, do you know the district minister of culture?"

"Er, yes, I do." Richard was stunned."

"I am the student he mentioned to you. We were on time. And this is my mother." The student turned to the older woman, who looked cautiously at Richard and nodded.

"Of course, of course. Welcome to America. Welcome to our city."

"Yes, we are glad to be here."

Richard reached towards the mother to shake hands. She hesitated and then shook his hand weakly. The daughter did the same.

"Let me help you with your bags." Richard reached for the mother's luggage.

"No, no, not necessary." She picked up both with ease.

They walked out of the station to the parking lot. Richard stared at William, who had a very perplexed expression on his face. William looked at Richard, who nodded slightly.

William immediately got out of the car with his hand outstretched. "Welcome, welcome."

Richard reacted quickly. "This is William. He is my colleague and mentor. We have known each other for some time."

"We are glad to meet you," they both said. "Should we put our bags in the back?"

"Yes, yes, in the trunk. Let me help you."

After several minutes of driving around the city to allow the new arrivals to see the sights, Richard broke the silence in an extra cheery tone. "Everything is going to work out wonderfully. We are going to the university reception center. They have a temporary room for you and will make arrangements for something more permanent. In the meantime, they will give you a pass to eat in their cafeteria. We know you must be tired and hungry after that long trip. Here is my telephone number and William's as well; they are our offices on campus. Contact us when you wish to."

"We assume you have all the necessary papers to let the receptionist know who you are," William broke in.

"Of course."

After parking and walking to the reception center, William turned to them. "I am going back to my office. I am very glad to have met you and hope to meet you again." He nodded. Richard watched him somewhat amused (almost looked like he bowed to them).

Richard accompanied them into the reception office and introduced them to the receptionist, who greeted enthusiastically. "We are glad you are coming to our university. We are sure you will enjoy your studies here."

Richard smiled at the receptionist. (thank goodness these people at the university are always so nice)

The receptionist looked at the mother. "And you are?"

"She is my mother," the student responded with a flash.

"You will be staying here as well?"

"Yes."

"I have only one bed in our guest room, but it is big enough for two people, so if you don't mind, I think it may work just fine."

Mother seemed comforted by the receptionist's concern. The receptionist looked up and smiled. "It won't be for more than a few days."

"Fine."

Heading for the door, Richard interrupted. "William and I would like to take you to lunch one of these days. Would that fit into your plans? We will leave a message here for you."

"Of course, we'd be delighted," Mother answered.

Richard headed immediately to William's office. "Well, old friend, life is full of surprises—in this case, a mother and daughter."

William shook his head. "Indeed. What do you think? Her mother must be real protective. Do you know what I think?"

"Yes, but tell me anyway."

"They'll stay and then after several months seek asylum. Their country is in a mess now. Great disorder. People trying to get out by the hundreds. Will be worse by winter."

"They don't seem wealthy. Where is the husband/father?"

"We may never know."

"Don't be so suspicious. We may learn much more later. I've invited them for lunch. I hope you can make it."

A day later at lunch, the conversation began as expected.

"What will you major in at the university?"

"Architecture, especially bridges," Student said. "I've always been interested in bridges. We have many ravines in our country and as children we always hoped to have bridges across them. It was so tiring having to climb up and down to get across the ravines. We spent endless time building little bridges."

Mother joined in. "Classes start in September, so we have time to read in the library."

"Yes, and work, too. Mother and I have asked for jobs in the cafeteria and it looks like they will need us."

William jumped in to change the subject. "Now that you have been in our country, what have you seen that is new to you? What surprises you?"

"Hmm," Student said pensively. Mother looked down at the floor and decided to keep quiet. "Well, what surprised me were the very big people here. I do not mean this big." she raised her hand over her head. "But this way." She raised her arms as if hugging a barrel. Mother threw her an angry look.

"Yes." Richard smiled. "We call them obese. I think part of the reason you will find them here is that our country produces very much food, all kinds of food, and this food is relatively cheap."

"Oh!" Student did not look convinced.

"Let me ask you a question." Richard looked directly at her. "Do you think people in your country would become big if they had so much food to eat that didn't cost much?"

"Of course!" Mother broke in and laughed for the first time.

Richard and William were surprised at her candor.

"Mother!"

"That's what I think," she and smiled broadly. "They'd eat like horses. Ha, ha. Why not?"

"What else surprises you?" Richard asked.

"Hmm," Student began. "Your dogs. I have never seen such spoiled dogs in my life. They are so clean; many look like they have been to the hairdresser. And their food; I have seen one side of a whole aisle in the supermarket with all kinds of dog food. Unbelievable!"

"Yes, people here love their dogs. What about your dogs? Do your people love them?"

"That's not the right word. They like them, but they also make their dogs work for them."

"In what manner?"

"They protect our flocks," Mother answered automatically.

"And they help us hunt wolves. I don't think your dogs work for a living. Do they?" Student went on the offensive.

"Most don't. On farms, I guess, if you want to call it that. For most people dogs are nice to have around. Oh, yes, in the city I guess they protect people in their apartments."

"Oh! From what?"

"From intruders or kidnappers."

"Yes, our radio has told us much about kidnapping in the U.S."

Richard was not ready for that comment, but pulled himself together (time to get a bit of humor in here). "We have a joke—-it says being obese is good because obese people are harder to kidnap."

Mother burst out in laughter. "That is funny, Mr. Richard. But," she hesitated, "It is not good manners."

"You are right. I will not tell that joke again."

Student did not hear the joke; she had been thinking quietly. "Let me say one more thing about our dogs."

"Yes."

"They have honor. They work hard. They do not get all the good food spoiled dogs get, and they protect us. That is honor."

William smiled. "Good point. Well, I must go now. Excuse me."

Everyone separated At least something was accomplished: they were getting to know each other a bit better.

In the following weeks, Student and Mother found a student apartment with shared bathroom facilities and kitchen in a small section of the city called Dinky Town. They loved that name and laughingly said to each other, "You are a Dinky Towner, I am Dinky Towner, not everyone is privileged to be a Dinky Towner."

Dinky Town was close to the university, had bookstores, small restaurants, and a café, which interestingly enough was the favorite of Richard and William. There was also a grocery and drug store where Student and Mother bought random items, like cheap perfume and a faux amber hairbrush.

The people who worked in Dinky Town were relaxed, friendly, and not inquisitive, and the many foreign students who lived there made Student and Mother feel very comfortable. This looked like a promising time for both of them. What freedom!

In a month, they bought two used bicycles for only ten dollars each and headed off like curious kids through the city. Wonderful! No military vehicles, very few policeman, no checkpoints. Classes were still months away, but they did take time to go to the library, each to a different section—Student to the architecture section, Mother to the engineering school library.

Weekends were special. They packed a lunch and headed toward the big river. They biked along it for miles, stopping at bridges on the way.

Outside the city to the south there were large bridges; more were located farther down where the river widened.

They stopped often by the first two large ones. Student sketched them from afar as well as up close. Mother inspected their construction—designs, materials, possible functions. Her desire to become a engineer was now being partially fulfilled.

A pleasant early summer month passed. They decided to invite Richard and William to the cafe for an afternoon coffee. Both readily accepted.

Richard entered the café, looked around, and thought to himself, 'The scene always changes and never changes—coffee drinkers looking in the distance—at a memory? At an image of the future? At nothing other than a street corner with a traffic light? A couple playing chess, several loners reading papers, smokers working crossword puzzles, and the perennial cluster of local conspirators thoughtfully sipping cappuccinos, talking about changing the world or at least rules of the university. Yes, Dinky Town has it.'

Student and Mother sat smiling in the back of the café. William came a few minutes later. "Well, here you are. I hope you two are now well settled."

"We are. I have been promoted to assistant manager in the cafeteria." Mother grinned. "I have already become important."

"Mother!"

Richard decided to fish for some ideas from them. "I am working on a problem concerning all humans."

William winced.

"Do you want to hear about it?" He looked at Student and Mother.

"Of course," they both said.

"It has to do with aggression—everyday aggression and also wars. So now I ask you, because I am interested in what people outside of our country think of war: what do you think causes wars and aggression in general?"

"There is too much of it." Mother said seriously.

"Yes, why?"

"Because, because . . ."

Student interrupted. "Because those who have little must take from those who have much. They have no choice."

"Take what?"

"Land, houses, money, everything they need to improve their lives."

William pursed his lips. "That is a very simplified explanation."

"That is all I can think of. We in our country know that is the way it is."

"Is there another way to solve this problem?" Richard warmed up to his own explanation.

"Yes. The rich and the poor should try to work things out peacefully. Cooperate and share."

"I agree, but some people fight even if they have enough to live on happily. Why?"

"Honor," Mother said. "For honor, for their beliefs, for what their religion asks them to do, to preserve their way of life, for the fact that they have been humiliated."

Student sat up straight. "I have not been here long enough to see what your country and people are like. I hope to see more so I can understand you better. We often fight to keep our traditions, to honor our dead, our heroes, our language. Do you?"

"We do," mused Richard. "But sometimes it's hard to see because there are so many different groups of people in the U.S."

"May I be so bold to change the subject? Mother interjected. "But what I have to say is not irrelevant to this conversation. Professor Richard, you were in our country; what surprised you about what you saw there?"

(William will love my answer) "Actually, not much. For the simple reason I was not there long enough and did not get to see much—I was working in schools most of the time. But your scenery was wild and wonderfully vast, and your people were polite and not very inquisitive." Richard paused a bit pensively. "I did have quite a bit of contact with your children, and they impressed me. They seemed glad to be in school; most were curious, had a good sense of humor, and were willing to learn. Some wanted me to give them presents—sweets or coins in my pocket, but others did not like that and felt it was impolite to ask visitors for presents."

"Were they like American children?"

"In my travels I've discovered that people all over acted in very similar ways in certain situations, despite the fact that many of their cultural practices were are different. I have found this especially true with young children. They do not have as much culture drilled into them as adults have. So my answer is that your children are, in important ways, like our children. But they also differ among themselves like children everywhere;

some are happy, some grumpy, some are leaders, some followers. But—and here is my unscientific bias—all children are wonderful and beautiful and innocent. And they should all be loved and treated fairly."

William winced and looked aside, as if to say, 'Too much Richard.'

Silence. Each averted eye contact with Richard. (so they are embarrassed . . . so what . . . it is true . . . I answered the question . . . now let William try to answer)

William didn't venture a response. He said he had to leave, and the coffee meeting came to a halt. Pleasantries were exchanged and everyone left the café. William and Richard went in different directions.

Several weeks later William called Richard. "Hey friend, I got a call from a common acquaintance—Mr. Security."

"What does he want?"

"He wants to meet us next Tuesday, 9:00 A.M., in my office. Can you make it?"

"Sure." (what does this mean . . . anything to do with my videotapes?)

On Tuesday, Mr. Security was already sitting in William's office when Richard arrived (looks like they have already been talking).

"Good morning," Richard said.

"Good morning, Professor Richard, did you get your tapes back yet?"

"No. Still time, though. Doesn't affect me much yet. I have much to do now to catch up with other things."

"I came as part of a routine check on people entering this country from abroad. You both know all about this routine. In this case, it has to do with the student and her mother who are here."

"Yes."

Mr. Security looked at Richard. "Nothing special about them. The young woman has a student visa, the mother a regular one. I don't know how they managed it; they may have applied some time ago—before things were getting a bit sticky between their country and ours. We like to know how they are doing. Student registered okay at the university?"

"Yes."

"The mother has a job in the cafeteria, the daughter as well, but part time. Is that correct?"

"Right." (who is feeding him this info?)

"Anything they do, their habits, that seem noteworthy?"

"Can't think of any. They spend a lot of time on the library, but otherwise, can't think of a thing." Richard appeared thoughtful.

"Oh yes," William said. "They like to ride their bicycles around town and along the river. The young one likes bridges; wants to be an architect and design bridges."

"The mother accompanies her?"

"Yes, she's interested in bridges, too, I guess."

"I see," Mr. Security said as he wrote something on a note pad.

"Okay then." He got up to go. "Thanks, gentlemen."

After Mr. Security left, William turned to Richard. "What do you think that was all about?"

"Routine check on foreign visitors, obviously," Richard replied a bit petulantly. (say no more)

"I guess it has to do simply with the fact that they still got visas when our current relations with that country are quite unstable," William surmised. "These are not the best times for a person from that part of the world to come to the U.S. It may be that there's something we don't know about."

"I hope it's not serious. They seem like fine people."

"Of course, of course, but as you well know, Richard, fine people can do bad things in bad times."

"Right, but not everyone."

"Okay, okay. See you later, Richard." (he thinks I'm still naive)

7

THE HELLS OF OCCUPATION

"WILLIAM HERE: I WAS at my home office writing, when Richard asked if he could visit me this evening after dinner. I had plans to finish a story for a prominent magazine. I had already passed the deadline, but Richard's voice sounded urgent so I relented. What are friends for?

After dinner, I sat in the den in my most comfortable chair next to the fire. I had a feeling it was going to be long, interesting evening. The bell rang and my daughter let Richard in."

"Greetings, William!" Richard was flushed with excitement. "I just got a long letter from an ex-student now teaching in Country Z. He is citizen of Z and is perfectly situated to do research there. He wants me to join him and will be my guide and collaborator. Country Z, as you know, has occupied the area some time ago and has a large population of indigenous people within its boundaries. These people are very dissatisfied with their lives and are becoming very unruly—sporadic strikes, acts of public violence, a deteriorating social scene in general."

"Not new, not new," William said. "An old story—colonial occupiers versus the occupied—both inhabiting roughly the same place, both struggling for a good life. History is replete with situations like that."

"Right," Richard continued. "This student became interested in my model of cooperation as a form of competition in the struggle for resources. He, like many of us in the field, believes that children gradually learn about this struggle early in their interactions with each other. They build up—mostly unconsciously, I presume—a core of very basic beliefs about justice and injustice. And what they learn throughout their early lives they ultimately apply to their own situations as adults. Anyway, that's what a lot of experts think and it's probably true. But, what scientific evidence do we have that it is true?"

"Yes, old story," William said. "Actually, two points to make about it: one, I agree a lot of folks think the connection is true, and, two, has the connection been tested adequately? Probably not."

"Right. Old problem. Now like most kids everywhere those in Z learn to compete within their families for what they want by squabbling with each other but also by sharing and cooperating. As they grow older, these children also learn to compete by deceiving, manipulating, and intimidating. You can recall these strategies from the study I did with the Fun-Cartoon Machine. Anyway, when they get older and situations get critical, children, now as adolescents, may resort to violence. Of course, they still share and cooperate with each other but usually not with strangers and certainly not with people they perceive to be their enemies."

"Makes sense. And?"

"Well, here's where my guide gets involved. He specializes in children's reasoning processes and is currently studying the effect of political and economic violence on their ability to deal with moral problems. His subjects are kids living in Z—kids of both the occupied and the occupiers. He wants to know whether these two groups of kids differ in their ways of coming up with moral answers posed by the occupation. He argues that the kids in the occupied areas should have a different sense of justice than kids of the occupiers. He feels that early deprivation and the negative experiences resulting from the occupation derails normal development toward cooperation and reciprocation and replaces it with resistance and aggression. The motivations behind it are driven by feelings of resentment and anger."

"All makes sense," William said.

"Right. To make it short, he feels the differences are in the way justice or injustice affect the way the children ultimately come to deal with the occupation as adults."

"You mean the kids in the occupied area should handle it badly—get angry sooner, use unfriendly tactics, etc. . . . A get-back-at-them kind of thing. Solution to the problem is aggression forcing restitution rather than negotiation and cooperation."

"Precisely," Richard said.

"Doesn't surprise me one bit. Where do you fit in?"

"I get the research money and I join him there and supervise the project. He has a colleague—a professor of clinical psychology—who lives in the occupied area. He will be my host. This professor has a broad and realistic understanding of the situation."

"And whose side is guide on?" William asked.

"Hard to tell. He is a citizen of Z but has many friends in the occupied area. For all I know, he may be neutral on the whole thing since he lived in Z most of his life and knows both sides."

"Could be very interesting, but . . ."

"I know what you're thinking. I will never get to the truth of the matter because neither side will show its true face; those interviewed will not tell the truth, and when parents find out what kind of research it is, they'll tell their kids what to say. And to make matters worse, it will be virtually impossible to get unbiased interviewers."

William nodded with confident assent. "Yes, and after you go to all that trouble and spend all that money, what will you come back with? Anything of scientific value? What you will come back with, frankly, is many untruths—some blatant, some subtle—mixed in with fewer truths. Richard, I am very appreciative of the fact that we can be blunt with each other. I wager you will come back with scientific junk. And in what form you yourself will come back will most likely be a matter of luck. The place is simply not safe."

"Could happen, but at least I will learn something. Nobody there can stop me from looking and listening. Just being there counts for something, even if I discover that everyone is not telling the truth, or at least not the whole truth. That itself is still a fact. There is a distinction between seeing and interviewing. Anyway, I will learn something and those who never go there will never know what the nature of that something is. Besides, if I talk to a lot of people, I'll at least get a bit closer to the truth than what the media offer. And when I return, I can then read up on the experiences of others who have been in the area, a kind of test of the validity of my observations."

"Perhaps," William said. "At least you're consistent. But...and this is always my parting word . . . you may get in trouble. Both sides may make trouble for you. Why wouldn't they? Both sides will see you as some kind of intruder or maybe an agent for the other side. Double the trouble. If you come back undamaged it may be just luck."

"That's the risk. But I am going."

"All right, but I warned you."

Two days after that conversation, Richard packed up and left the country with one suitcase and a backpack of research forms.

In the U.S. airport waiting area, he got off to a bad start. A huge and restless elderly man sitting next to Richard began telling him his life history. He had experienced terrible things in his early life in Z, but he loved his country. "If it were not for those other people who live there—those animals—they make trouble all the time against us and amongst themselves. They should be driven out like vermin."

Richard quickly inferred 'they' were the occupied. His sympathy for the man suddenly vanished and his anger mounted. Calling people animals is the first step toward killing them. "You sound like a racist!" (what in the world am I saying . . . what an insult . . . never insult a stranger . . . Richard, you're stupid)

The man almost exploded and made a fist. He hesitated and then turned his back to Richard—end of friendly conversation. The man's frightened wife sat fretfully next to him.

As Richard was getting into line to board the plane, the man reached up and grabbed Richard by his arm. Pain and embarrassment spread across his face. Richard's emotions were just as mixed. The man reached out to shake Richard's hand. Richard hesitated, then shook his hand. (peace brother . . . but no peace brother . . . don't you know hatred brings more hatred?)

About twenty minutes later Richard's emotions underwent another change. A friendly young man sitting next to him on the plane was also from Country Z. He was a scientist working temporarily in the U.S. In conversation about Z, the young man casually said he didn't know anyone from the occupied area, but thought they were probably like everyone else and he hoped to live in peace with them. (amazing he doesn't know those people even though they live next to him . . . this trip is really going to be interesting . . . and complicated)

Going through the checkpoint was easy. Before leaving, Richard's guide had supplied him with a letter written by his own department head of the university in the occupied country. The letter was an invitation to Richard to participate in the research project. As Richard learned earlier, this was a good move. Official letters are always a traveler's best friend. The checkpoint official looked at it and approved. (so far, I am a good boy)

A student of Richard's guide met him at the airport (why his student . . . why not Guide himself ?). They chatted briefly and then went outside where Guide was waiting.

"Welcome, welcome. Had a good flight?"

"Yes, good to be here."

Riding in Country Z was a treat. Smooth roads, impressive houses, small, well-groomed parks, smartly dressed people—affluence and organization at their best. Guide rattled on for several miles. "The project will be 'great'; it will work out 'super'. Do you have the money?" "Yes."

"We will exchange it when we get there."

When they got close to the border of the occupied area, Guide said, "Now it could get complicated, but it will work out."

"Sure. Why not? We're friendly and innocent academics."

Things went smoothly at the first checkpoint. The first official was sullen, clearly bored by the routine. But as they approached the second official the situation changed; he unexpectedly asked Richard, "You have only a U.S. passport?"

"Yes. I just showed it to your colleague back there." Richard pointed back to the official.

"Yes, I saw that. But you," he pointed to Guide, "you also have a U.S. passport. But I just saw you put another passport in your pocket."

"Yes, I have two passports—one for our country and one from the U.S."

"Are you two together?"

"Yes."

"You," he addressed Richard, "you go over there." He pointed to a group of soldiers.

"Yes, sir." (the boss is always right . . . but what's the problem?)

The official turned to Guide. "You stay here".

Guide burst into anger. "I must stay with him. I am his host." The official ignored him. Guide started yelling at the official who was immediately joined by an armed guard. The official retorted sharply. Guide retorted even more sharply.

Richard understood none of what they were saying. In seconds, there was much yelling back and forth. It sounded like insults. But Richard found it interesting because it also sounded somewhat routine.

Suddenly the official called to one of the soldiers standing near Richard. He motioned to take Richard to the crossing point. The soldier said to Richard in broken English, "You, VIP, come with me."

Richard looked at Guide who was still yelling and then turned and dutifully followed the soldier (good start . . . first time in my life I am VIP)

After walking alone across a no-man's land—a gravel road surrounded by concrete walls topped with razor wire—Richard was greeted by an official from the occupied side. He was casually dressed, carried a pistol in a tattered holster, and seemed tired. He looked quickly at Richard's passport. "Okay."

Richard kept walking straight ahead until he got beyond what looked like the last guardhouse. No one was around. (now what?)

He walked over to the concrete wall, took off his backpack, and sat down on the dirt road with his back against the wall. It was getting dark. "Great start!" he muttered out loud. (might as well try to get some sleep)

After about half an hour, a tall, thin man came up to him. "You, professor psychology?"

Richard nodded. (why not?)

"You wait here."

Richard did and it got colder. About an hour later a rattling, rust-blotched car appeared. Richard got up stiffly. The professor of clinical psychology emerged from the car.

"Welcome, Professor Richard. I am sorry I am late, but sometimes things do not move quickly here. I am your host. Your guide has informed me of everything on his cell phone. Please come with me to my house."

The house was fairly large but modest. Seven family members were brought into the doorway. They greeted Richard politely, then without another word, disappeared. The professor invited Richard to a separate room with a large table. A young girl and the professor's wife brought in two large platters of food.

"This is very kind of you," Richard said to his host. "But it is too late for all of you to go to the trouble. It's going on midnight."

"It is no trouble."

Richard ate in silence glancing occasionally at his host and smiling in appreciation. The food was good and he was very hungry. The professor sat across from him grinning faintly. (what can he be thinking?)

Richard looked up at him. "You know about our research plan?"

(best to get down to business immediately . . . he has to follow our procedures exactly . . . otherwise the data will be compromised)

"Yes," his host smiled. "It is very interesting."

"As you know, this is a scientific study, so we must follow strict procedures for carrying it out." (this is not a nice way to start off with such a gracious host but I have to . . . but does this guy know what I am getting at?)

"Of course, of course."

"I ask this because researchers may be trained differently in different countries."

"Possibly, but not here. We have the same scientific methods as you do."

"Fine." (I wonder) "You have six students to assist us? We also have six students doing interviews on the other side."

"Yes."

"Do they know how to conduct unbiased interviews? And are they aware that someone else will be conducting a similar interview—at least the basic questions—with the same person at another time, so we can check on reliability?"

"Of course."

(really?) "We will pay them for their efforts. As soon as I exchange our money, I will give you money to pay them when they complete their interviews." Richard preferred to reward those who do the hard work. (avoid middlemen as much as possible)

"Fine."

"Now, for reasons I need not go into it is important that each interview protocol will be given a number, but not the name of the person interviewed. The name and a corresponding number will be recorded on a master list containing all those participating in the study. This list will be given only to me. I will keep it separate from the interview protocols at the end of the study."

"Of course. I see nothing objectionable to this."

After a few more queries and instructions on how to conduct the interviews, Richard yawned.

The professor smiled. "It is late and you must be very tired. May I show you your room?"

Richard had a difficult time sleeping. The next morning he awoke to a strange world outside his window. It was a cramped city of hundreds of concrete-block houses—one story with steel reinforcing bars sticking up from their roofs. They were built in preparation for the second story to come. The city was clearly unfinished and shell-damaged. Streets were a mixture of broken concrete and gravel. Carts rattled loudly as vendors pushed and pulled them over the rough surfaces. Adults were poorly dressed but had a confident bearing. Children were cleanly dressed and played in the street and on piles of construction materials.

The next day, Guide appeared in a good mood (as if nothing happened). "All is well. I could not join you last evening, but here I am. Now we must first go to an important man who will give us a letter so we can move about this town without inconvenience. He is a general in the armed forces and has his office in the prison."

Richard and Guide were accompanied into the prison. After being questioned several times by guards and asked to show two forms of identification, they were led through concrete halls by two grim armed men. After seventy-three paces and two turns to the right (Richard planned an escape route) they came to the general's office.

An aide opened the door and let them in. The room had heavy green drapes hanging on the walls—no windows, only one other door. Off to the side was a small sofa and two chairs clustered around a low table holding tea cups and what looked like a sugar bowl and a metal plate of cookies. The general sat off on a bigger chair nearby. He got up slowly as if in pain and smiled. He was missing an eye and had a cane leaning against his chair.

"Welcome, Professor Richard. I am delighted to see you and happy that you are doing research in our country. I did have some science courses before studying history and after that I turned to the military. But I did a similar scientific study as yours (what a coincidence!) with the help of my assistant." He gestured toward a young, somewhat dapper, officer who nodded to Richard with a big smile.

"I am sure you will be interested in our study. I will give it to you the next time you visit me. I think you will find it useful."

"Thank you." (what could it really be about . . . can't be like ours)

The general then brightened up. "I have been to your country years ago—actually to your city and even to your university. I gave a talk there, however, no one came to hear me except students from our own country. They did not to have to hear my talk, but they were glad to see me. But why students from your country did not come to hear me speak is fuzzling. In this country, all students go to hear speakers from the outside. They are less boring than speakers from their own country. Ha, ha."

"Yes, it is puzzling. Perhaps they were not notified in time."

Guide then interrupted. "The general has been to Dinky Town."

"What?" Richard burst out laughing. "Dinky Town! What a coincidence! That is a wonderful place near the university. Guide and I planned this trip there in that cafe."

"I know that cafe. It was very comfortable." Then general paused and appeared thoughtful. "May I tell you a bit about the history of this country?"

"Of course." (does he have time for this?)

Fifteen minutes later the general's history lesson was brought to an unexpected halt by his assistant.

"Excuse me, but we will be late for an appointment."

"Oh, yes." The general struggled to get up. "I hope we can meet again to continue my history lesson," he laughed. "I hope your visit here goes well. I have an official letter for you to account for the significance of your work here. It will help you."

He turned to his assistant who handed Richard the letter. "I wish you luck with your research and hope to get a copy of the results when it is completed. Oh, yes, I hope we will also have time in the future to talk about the results. For that you will have to come back here again. You will like it even better the second time."

"Yes, of course. That would be very enjoyable." (I'm not so sure about that)

Just as they proceeded out the door, the assistant stepped toward Richard. "Excuse me. You are a child psychologist. I have a question about my son."

"Yes, I am, but I am not a clinical psychologist—I am only a research psychologist."

"That's okay. But my son hangs on to his mother a lot and often does not come to me when I call. He cries instead."

"Do you spend much time with your son?"

"As much as I can, but it is difficult. I am always so busy."

"How old is he?"

"He is two and a half. A fine boy. He will be big and strong, but his mother—he hangs on her too much."

"I think that is not bad. I think, maybe when you have more time with him and play with him more, he will become your best friend." Richard smiled.

The aide also smiled. "It has been good to talk to you."

Meanwhile, the general stood by, leaning heavily on his cane and smiling genially.

They all shook hands and Richard and Guide went into the hall followed by two guards. (good guys, but what a place to have an office . . life must really be tough around here)

After getting out onto the street, Richard went immediately with Guide to a nearby bank to exchange money. He had no idea what was happening at the cashier's window. After several minutes he and Guide left. He had two envelopes bulging with bills. He wondered how much the bank made on this one. He was totally in the dark. "As long as we can pay the students a fair amount," he said to Guide, who was almost joyously folding a large handful of bills into his wallet.

The next day Richard and the professor met the student assistants. Two of them appeared tired (looks like they are malnourished); another was more energetic but quiet; the fourth spoke very good English and took over the role of leading the others. "Two more are late, but they will come," the professor said.

Richard was strongly motivated to ask them about their schooling and their plans for the future, but refrained. He would wait until they finished their interviews with the children. Instead they wanted to know which American pop singer was his favorite.

"Well, I don't listen much to entertainers. I guess all of them are pretty good." He kept looking at their facial skin. (vitamin deficiency?)

They were clearly disappointed with his answer.

He then went to a local family with the professor, who was well received. Many family members came into the living room. The professor made all the introductions. The oldest man in the family, presumably the father, offered tea.

The rest of the family members were quiet and politely waited for Guide to start the conversation. Guide made some standard introductory remarks and then talked about the research with the children. The adults nodded. They seemed to understand what the research was about.

Then Richard entered the conversation and from the moment he started, he was sorry. "Yes, we study competition for things people need

But competing is often not just and justice is not easy to get when people disagree."

The father smiled. "You mean here?"

"Yes." (just opened Pandora's box . . . how stupid of me)

"Well, living under occupation puts us at a great disadvantage. You can see it already, can't you?"

"Yes. I understand." Richard knew this was not a good answer.

"I hope you do. Let me expand your understanding." The elderly lady in the room, presumably his wife, put her hand gently on his arm and said something under her breath.

"Excuse me sir, my wife is right. It is not necessary to talk about these things. Excuse me."

Richard looked straight at him. "But it is necessary for me to know. As a scientist, it is important to know how people live. When I go home, people will ask me and what will I say? 'I know no more than a tourist just passing through.' Sir, I am more than a tourist. As you know, tourists are led only to see the pleasant things of the countries they visit—the monuments, the historical sites, happy citizens enjoying their life. They see only the nice picture painted by the tourist agency and they only visit places local officials arrange for them to see. I do not like that. I did not come all this way to be told what to see."

The father looked at him and smiled.

What followed was a slowly building torrent of stories and comments from everyone in the room. "The occupation is very hard on all of us, especially the children. Schools are often closed because of violence. We cannot travel freely, police do random visits, sometime inside our houses at three in the morning."

"Wait." Richard almost got up. "When they come into houses what do they do?"

"Ah, ha. They first tell the father in the house to sit down and keep quiet. And if he interferes, he will lose his job."

"Then what? "

"Then, they ask who is the oldest son."

"And then what?" (this is getting terrible)

"Then they take him and break his . . . "

The man's wife screamed something Richard could not understand.

"What, what does the father do?" (what a terrible question . . . but)

There was a long silence. "He smokes." The father swallowed hard and looked away.

Then a daughter spoke up. "If the occupiers need to clear buildings near our railroad, they tell the owners to leave and knock their houses down."

"Wait. Wait. Why do the occupiers do this?"

"Ha, because they do not like us! Because we make life as hard for them as we can because this is our home. It was our home, but we cannot get it back. We are not strong enough. We do not have enough big guns."

An older boy interrupted. "We need more guns to do it."

"Chah!" The mother said sharply.

He continued. "We do everything we can to hurt them, so they are afraid of us. But they are occupying our country. Of course, we try to avoid getting caught. If we get caught, they torture us."

"I understand this." Richard got flushed. "But they, too, have to defend themselves."

An adolescent son raised his hand. "They break your fingers."

"Leave the room," the mother barked to her children. She sat down stoically and looked straight ahead.

Richard stared with great admiration at her for a fraction of a second, hoping she wouldn't see him. (women hold everything together)

"You think we are unreasonable? "the father asked Richard.

"No, but . . . "

"You cannot understand. No one outside here will ever understand. We will die here like animals if nothing changes. Look, we already are beginning to act like animals. We yell at each other, and some neighbors have starting fighting with each other. Soon we will kill each other. This place is becoming an insane asylum and the occupiers know it and want more of it. It weakens us."

He paused, gripped by anger.

"You ask the children about justice. Yes, that is what we want, but we won't get it until we fight for it, die for it. Mankind has been doing that for centuries. Your forefathers fought for their freedom and won; your Indians fought and lost. You must know that."

"I do, but we . . . "

"Cooperating with the occupation is dead."

Richard was overcome with a bleakness he had never felt in his life. (no hope . . . no damn hope . . . guns . . . more killing . . . more death . . .

69

one side should make concessions . . . .should share . . . maybe one side should pack up and leave, but to where?)

Richard suddenly stood up. "I am very sorry, very sorry. I must go now." He turned to Guide who sat through the whole ordeal without saying a word. (as if to tell me 'I told you so')

Everyone in the room stood up. He and the father shook hands. The others faded back. Richard looked at the young children. (gotta control the tears)

He turned to the father. "Is there anything I can do?"

"Tell this story when you get home."

Outside on the street, Richard said to Guide. "Money. They can have all my money."

"We will discuss that later."

When they left, Richard forgot to say goodbye. (what a debacle!)

The next day, Richard insisted on going back. The mother answered the door. The father was not there. Richard greeted her.

"I have something for the children. For the children. You must understand, I am a friend of your children." He handed her an envelope. "Please take it. It is for the children. From my country to your country."

She hesitated.

Guide looked at her with a smile. "Aren't you supposed to make your visitors happy?"

She smiled, but did not put out her hand.

Guide looked sternly at the mother. "It is a custom of his people in America to help children. You must respect their custom. Take it."

She hesitated. "Thank you." She took it awkwardly.

Richard wanted to kiss her on the forehead, but then stopped. (are you crazy?)

Subsequent visits to families were less dramatic, but the message became clear: life here had become a hell. No matter if anyone in the U.S. did not know it. He now knew it. He wondered if William did as well.

A depressing week later, Richard struck out on his own and went to the capital city to be alone. He was getting desperate. It was Sunday and he found a mission church and made mass on time. It calmed him down. There were well-dressed tourists in church. Richard wondered what they had seen of the country.

Outside on a small street of shops and cafes, Richard began feeling better. Civilization. Peace.

Then the sense of peace exploded. A young man pushing a cart of vegetables was stopped by two policemen; one stood off to the side armed with a pistol. They were spotlessly dressed—clean, starched uniforms—and wore leather gloves. They were checking the vendor's papers and seemed to find them unsatisfactory. (was he illegally selling his vegetables?)

The interrogating policeman then folded one of the vendor's documents and put it into a slim leather brief case he held under his arm. The vendor yelled out something. As he reached to retrieve the document, the policeman smiled and turned around. The armed policeman moved between him and the vendor. Case closed! Complain all you want!

Already boiling, Richard was ready to confront the police, but then stopped (what good would it do? . . . they would not listen). His old trick of trying to embarrass the police to change their minds in front of curious tourists would never work in this case. And it could make things worse for the vendor.

Richard went over to the vendor. He was about 19 or 20 and wore a ragged shirt and patched pants. For a split second, he seemed on the verge of crying. Richard awkwardly reached out to him. "Sir, I am your friend. You understand, I am your friend." He reached for his wallet. "Here. This will show you."

Without warning, the vendor slapped Richard's hand away.

Richard was startled and embarrassed (wrong again, that'll teach me). He raised both hands and walked away (and this day had such a good start). Little did he expect it would get worse.

As he was leisurely walking past shops and souvenir stalls, trying to calm down, he noticed a reflection in a shop window; it was of a young man walking about six paces behind him. Richard had seen him two or three times already. A coincidence? (seems like he's tailing me . . . gotta watch him)

Richard stopped suddenly at a shop window and watched for the man's reaction in the reflection. He was thin and ascetic looking. (could be student, or a beggar, or both)

The young man fluidly slid past Richard and kept going. Richard waited, then followed him (prey follows hunter). The man turned off abruptly into an alley. Richard kept straight ahead. (could be wrong about him . . . but then that's a common maneuver . . . we'll see)

About two minutes later, Richard checked for him in a store window reflection (still there . . . .no coincidence . . . probably a pick pocket . . .

won't get anything . . . money and passport in my chest pouch . . . hanky in side pocket . . . backpack buckled tightly)

Richard picked up the pace. The man did as well. Suddenly, he quickly moved up to Richard. Richard felt slight pressure on his backpack and stopped suddenly to look in a store window. The man abruptly walked past Richard. (a pickpocket)

About five minutes later at the edge of the shopping area two boys in the middle of the sidewalk approached Richard. "Want a soft drink, sir?"

"Sure." Richard stopped. At that moment, one of the boys yelled out. "Watch out, sir, he's a thief!" Richard spun around and suddenly faced the young man who had been following him.

Without hesitating, Richard reached out and grabbed him by his neck and collar and yelled like a maniac, "Stop! I am police! You understand police? I will take you to the authorities!"

The young man looked at him impassively. He showed no fear, not even resignation (he's on drugs). Richard stared into his face, trying to appear very angry (what the hell am I doing?). He then released his grip on his neck. "Get out!" The young man did not move. Richard walked away.

Richard picked up his pace and entered a fast-moving stream of pedestrians. He moved quickly along with them and was tripped several times by several other young men (intentional? . . . or?). But he didn't slow down and didn't care (if they all want trouble I'll give it to them). For the first time in a long time, Richard was angry and feeling paranoid.

He remembered the street that turned off to the International Club and headed for it. The walkers thinned out. He felt his spirits coming back. (now for a cool glass of beer and some jottings in my journal)

He got quickly to the beer, but not the journal. As he settled down, it dawned on him that he was becoming just like the place—angry and nasty. (could have done something much better than grabbing that man and trying to choke him . . . I'm acting like everyone else around here)

The next day, Guide informed Richard that the project on the other side of the border was moving along well—everyone was cooperative but it was too early to say anything about them. Initially, it appeared the occupiers' children were friendly and for negotiating differences, while the children of the occupied were more vindictive and emotional. (fits the theory . . . but still the possibility a bias in interviewing can creep in . . . but no way to stop it).

While the interviews continued, a soft-spoken relative of Guide appeared and offered to drive Richard around the country to see the sights. "It was perfectly safe," he told Richard. "I teach children geography, so I know this area well."

The drive took them through rural areas—fields and small plantations of walnut trees. They stopped at one plantation owner's home. He and the teacher were good friends. They greeted Richard graciously. The children were especially friendly; they wanted to know everything about America. When Richard got ready to leave, the owner gave him a cloth bag of walnuts. "I am sure you will enjoy them sir." Richard found them delicious but different from those he ate at home. "Thank you, thank you very much."

"Give our greetings to America."

"Yes, I will, and I would like to give you something but I have nothing with me."

"Your visit was enough."

On the return trip Richard tried to learn more about the country, but the answers he got were surprisingly short. Those he got were about the weather and the landscape, nothing about the political situation.

Richard wondered why (doesn't trust me. . . thinks I am a spy?). This suspicion was reinforced shortly later when they stopped at another relative's house. A group of six or seven young men were standing in the garden smoking and chatting. They were most likely out of a job and seemed bored and restless—a bit menacing. For a second, Richard thought there could be trouble.

They were polite, asked few questions, and talked about the obvious. But they were curious about Richard's research. Sooner or later, he felt they would get into politics. His driver must have sensed it coming. "We must be off," he said.

Several days later, the interviews were completed. Richard picked up the protocols, checked their contents, saw that each one was numbered and found no personal names of those interviewed. Some of the writing was illegible. Guide said he'd check on it when he got back to the U.S. Richard felt uncomfortable—he was scheduled to leave the country the next day, but he wanted to be certain the interview subjects were not identified. He also went through his journal and made sure that no individual names were on it—only code names like "Mr. Dinkey Town," and

"Mrs. Great Cook." (I'm really getting paranoid . . . playing spy . . . .all this is probably harmless . . . but can't be sure)

Guide gave him a list of those interviewed and their corresponding code numbers. Richard put the list into his chest pouch next to his passport and plane ticket. (don't want to make trouble for those in the study . . . authorities always interested in possible subversives . . . I can leave but they cannot)

After a sad goodbye to the professor's family (will we ever meet again), Richard and the professor rode to the checkpoint separating the occupied area from the rest of the country. Then the professor unexpectedly said in a strangely matter-of-fact tone, "I hope your intelligence agency will learn something from your research."

(what . . . what does that mean) "I don't under . . . yes, of course, if they ask for it." (what has he been thinking all this time?)

8

GETTING CAUGHT

ON HIS WAY TO the airport, Richard sifted through his mixed feelings about the visit. He enjoyed seeing the country but had a deep sense of anger and fear that there was something ominous going on there. (when they reach adulthood will these children someday fight each other to death . . . ? will this whole place be destroyed . . . ? justice cannot be violated for ever)

The airport was in turmoil. Security officers were searching every waste container and requiring passengers to take all their luggage and wait in specified areas.

When the time came for the passengers to line up for check-in, Richard waited to assess which of the five officials checking passengers was the "easiest." As it turned out, he could not decide. They all seemed immune to anyone who may have wanted to get by easily. (okay . . . which one?)

His choice was made for him. At the far end, the official motioned brusquely for Richard to come over. (shouldn't have come so early . . . more passengers around would have given me more time to choose . . . I don't like this guy)

"Passport and ticket please." He looked at it carefully. "Purpose of your visit?"

"To see your country and also to do research with children. I work with children living in countries all over the world."

"Hmm. Where have you stayed while you were here?"

"At a number of places. I traveled around a lot."

"I see here," he pointed to some marks at the bottom of Richard's visa, which had been stapled to his passport, "that you have been to the occupied area." (I didn't see them do that)

"Yes, I have, because we did research there as well as in your area."

75

"Who is 'we'?"

'My guide, a citizen of your country, and a young faculty member of your university."

"Hmm. And the places you stayed at?"

"Strangely, I don't exactly remember the names of them. Foreign languages are a problem for me."

"You are a professor, and you don't remember names and places. I am surprised. How can a professor have such a poor memory?" (you jerk)

"Surely, you must understand about absent-minded professors. I sometimes think so abstractly I usually forget names of places and people. Names are arbitrary, but good theories are not. Good scientific theories are coherent and compelling, never arbitrary like people's names. I am sure you know this as well." (don't get sassy)

No reaction. (stone-face . . . you are a bureaucratic jerk . . . and dangerous)

The official put his left hand inadvertently on Richard's backpack, the one bulging with the interview documents. (you're close man . . . but you're never going to get to see them . . . if I can help it).

"Who gave you permission to do this research?"

"Our government and your university."

"Who at our university?"

"The man who wrote this letter." Richard pulled out his letter of invitation and pointed to the letterhead and the signature name at the bottom. Then he had a horrible thought (suppose it was faked). He waved it slowly past the official's face but then pulled it away. (not too fast)

The official glanced. "Do you keep a journal?"

"I do." Richard flared in anger. "And you will not see it. It is private. I thought this was a civilized country."

The official blanched, composed himself, and before he could re-cover, Richard inexplicably pointed to the bag of walnuts sticking out of his backpack. "You should have one of these. I tasted them and they are delicious." (that was stupid)

The official studied Richard's eyes. (the chancellor)

Richard returned the look (the final test, you b . . . . st . . . .rd) and involuntarily turned his head. The room was empty.

The official glanced at his watch. "You may go."

Richard picked up his backpack and suitcase and walked away.

(beat ya, ya s . . . n . . . f . . . b . . . tch)

In the waiting area Richard sat tensely with his back to the wall. (sometimes they change their minds)

On the plane, he waited to breath until the door was slammed shut and locked. (whew . . . gotta stop doing this)

9

DINNER AND DISCLOSURE

AFTER RICHARD GOT BACK from the occupied country, he immediately looked at his protocols and found many of them difficult
to evaluate. He tried to get measures of agreement between answers to
similar interview questions, but was not successful. Also, some answers
appeared too perfunctory, thus suggesting some bias, but then that does
not necessarily follow. There was still, however, sufficient observational
material and anecdotal information to justify a brief article on his experience. William was right: the trip was not an unadulterated scientific
success. But Richard learned things he never knew before. That made it
all worthwhile.

By now it was early autumn, almost one year since Student and
Mother arrived in the U.S. During the year they had many good moments together in their new surroundings. The university classes turned
out very useful for Student; she made several friends, and was enjoying
her life in the U.S. more than she anticipated. Mother was promoted to
cafeteria manager and spent many hours improving their apartment. She
had friendly neighbors and enjoyed her time in the library reading metal-
lurgy journals.

In the middle of all these activities, Mr. Security came by Richard's
office to "keep updated."

"How are your visitors doing, Professor Richard?"

"Fine. They are well-settled. The student is doing great in her classes
and her mother is very satisfied with her job. Why do you ask?"

Ignoring his question, Mr. Security looked directly at Richard.
"Anything they're doing seem out of the ordinary to you?"

Richard hesitated. "No, but I don't know everything they're doing.
Why do you ask?"

"A routine question. We're checking on the activities of everyone coming into this country for an extended visit. Standard procedure."

"I have seen nothing that appears suspicious. Oh, yes, they do ride around on their bicycles quite a bit, but we already told you this."

"What do you mean?"

"They take daytrips, sometimes two a day, along the Great River." (why be interested in their free time . . . unless)

"Oh." Mr. Security's hesitated a moment. "By the way, did you ever get your tapes back?"

"No."

"Okay, let's keep in touch." He got up abruptly and left.

Two days later, Student and Mother invited Richard and William to dinner—their first dinner guests in the U.S. They were excited and had great fun planning the menu, shopping, setting the table, and making extra trips to buy wine and flowers for the table.

They got their preparations done half an hour before their guests arrived and sat down to think over the things to say to their hosts about their stay in the U.S. They felt obligated to give them more than just a superficial we-enjoyed-it-very-much answer. Just before Richard was to leave his office for dinner, his secretary laid an envelope on his desk. "Just arrived. No return address. Looks foreign."

He opened it.

"Dear Professor Richard,

I am delighted you have hosted our student. It is important at times like this that both our peoples maintain personal, cultural, and economic ties regardless of political differences.

As for our past meeting at our airport—I was about to send you your videotapes with the student, but felt they may hamper her entry into your country. I have looked at them and found some of their content interesting, but I admit I did not look at them completely. Frankly, I found them boring.

(good . . . so he may not have discovered the other shots . . . but maybe he had and is just keeping quiet about them)

Now I have been thinking about you coming to our country to finish the last stage of your research—if I understand it, to teach children the value of cooperation.

Because you have expressed interest in working with children all over the world (you can see I do not forget interesting ideas even after a year) to pursue your valuable research with the Fun-Cartoon Machine, I officially invite you to come here and work with our children. I have discussed this with our government officials and they consented to this plan and even offered to support it. They were a bit puzzled about the effects your effort would have on our children, but they felt no harm would come to them. Of course, like most people here, my guess is they feel that trying to teach children to work cooperatively is somewhat a waste of time. Like adults, children learn quickly to do whatever the situation requires.

Our political situation, as you must know, is a bit unstable at the moment. But we assure you will not have difficulties. You will be working in schools a good distance from the troublemakers who are relatively few in number and located south of our city.

Unfortunately, we cannot provide financial assistance for your flight, but we can provide room, meals, and transportation. Fall is a good time here. Winter, however, can move in quickly and be a bit challenging. But you will most likely finish your work by then.

I hope you will accept this invitation in the spirit of goodwill that can and should be maintained between our countries.

Respectfully yours,

District Minister of Culture

(whew . . . now what?)

William suddenly appeared at the door. "Hi William!" Richard jumped up and casually folded the letter and put it in his pocket. "We're off to dinner. Should be interesting."

Their hosts were genuinely happy to see them. "Come in, come in."

"Finally."

"The weather is wonderful."

"Yes. It is wonderful."

Small talk. This could be very boring, William thought. To his surprise, though, the food turned out to be quite exciting and exotic. Before long, the two guests could not stop raving about it. A bottle of wine was consumed without anyone noticing. A second bottle was opened and the conversation became even more animated.

Richard then remembered an earlier conversation. "I don't know if you remember but some time back one of you asked me what I learned about your country. As you know, I was there for only a short period of time. On the bus trip to the school, I had a chance to observe a lot of people on the bus and at different bus stations. They struck me as mostly poor but well-adjusted and dignified. The children in school were attentive to me and the Fun-Cartoon Machine. They quickly comprehended what the cartoon game was all about and eagerly went to it. The more I got to know them, the more I liked them.

They behaved like all the kids I have worked with so far. A colleague of mine who studies people from various cultures has discovered that no matter how different the cultures are from each other, their peoples share many similar behavior patterns. This is especially true of children. Also, not surprising perhaps, is the fact that people within a particular culture differ from each other in the same way that people in other cultures differ. This may not be an astounding finding, but it does explain things about many social interactions within a culture. Some children are leaders, some followers, some active, some passive, some jolly, some depressed. I am sure you have also seen this."

Richard was trying desperately to get them to respond to this finding and see its relationship to his upcoming project. But the response was polite silence.

"My impressions of your country are probably not surprising to you, but they are important for my theory. I hope to incorporate them in my final report. I think that first-hand impressions, even though anecdotal, are useful—along with data, of course—in science. The informal can always expand and enrich the formal. As far as I can determine, the major finding—namely the universality of many basic elements of human nature and behavior—has not been sufficiently recognized as a key concept in educating children. Recognizing universal traits makes it possible to view all people as having the same needs, desires, and problems. This means we can all look at each other as relatives despite our many different customs and languages."

"I totally agree," William broke in. "At least that part. But we should not forget that talents and skills for survival may favor some groups over others. Why? For many reasons, like unpredictable natural events and economic conditions. The amount of rainfall can make one group of farmers rich and another group very poor. And the disparity in wealth that results can lead to dissatisfaction and ultimately to some form of conflict. At the bottom, much of history is due to sheer luck."

"Yes, but let me continue." Richard did not want to lose the chain of his impressions of their country. "I did see quite a few officials, mostly at the airport and some of them impressed me as quite competent. Take your minister of culture: he impressed me as quite an educated man, and quite astute. He, as you know, felt obligated to keep my videotapes, but I'm sure he will return them." (there . . . the bait is on the table)

"Yes, yes," Mother interrupted. "He is an educated man and he does his job well." (she seems to have no idea about the tapes)

As the dinner proceeded the conversation became increasingly lively. Even William was having fun, and with every sip of wine he realized these ladies were smarter that he originally thought. Realizing he (not William, for a change) was getting a bit too academic, Richard nevertheless continued lecturing on his impressions—this time on those of the U.S.

"And you ask me—perhaps you don't remember—what I feel about our own country. Of course, our country has its problems—no country is free of them—but in general people here try to be fair to each other, often to those who are disadvantaged. Also, there are thousands of charities in the U.S., more, I believe, than anywhere else in the world. And these charities are supported by rich and poor people.

People here, in general, also obey the laws, although cheating on money matters seems to have increased lately. But when this happens on a high level, our lawyers and courts get after them. Even our highest official can be called into court and tried, if necessary."

Richard hesitated. "As for foreigners, many Americans, especially those living outside large cities, do not know many foreigners, other than migrant workers and the relatively few they meet when they tour other countries. Most read about foreigners in magazines and newspapers, or see them television when there are wars or catastrophes." (enough . . . they are getting bored)

Bothered by Richard's prolonged lecture, William did not want to be left out. "Yes, yes, and don't forget language. Unlike many peoples in foreign countries, Americans mostly speak only one language—English. In most countries I have visited many people speak at least two languages, one of which is English. You two are good examples, and I am very impressed with how well you speak our language."

"I am, too," Richard agreed. (William is really getting congenial . . . I'll have a secret toast to that)

"Not only that." William smiled broadly and allowed himself what his hosts felt was an unecessary non sequitor. "I am also impressed with how you prepare a meal for guests."

Richard looked at him. (the wine for sure)

After several minutes of such fun talk, a shadow unexpectedly fell over the table. Student was visible bothered by something. Then, the bombshell.

"Mother," Student turned to Mother. "I'm not going back home!"

"What? What do you mean?"

"Just that. I'm staying here. I made friends here and my grades are good. I love what I'm studying."

"What? You can't! Your visa will run out. You don't have any authority to stay here! You're talking nonsense."

"No. I'm not." She turned to Richard and William. "You should know something very important: my father is in jail. Protective custody, they say. The government claims it is protecting him. Ha, ha! That is an outright lie. They are afraid of him. He writes things about freedom and justice, so they have to stop him."

"Quiet!" Mother yelled at Student with a mixture of fear and anger. "No more!"

"It's okay," Richard said to Mother. "What she says here is totally confidential; it will never be mentioned by us to anyone. It's important for her to make her feelings clear and we should hear her reasons now that she has made such a big decision."

"My going back will never help my father. My staying here may. I am going to appeal to an amnesty group to have him released as a prisoner of conscience—a person of no threat to his country. I have already talked to people on campus as to how this can be done. I have not mentioned father specifically, though. I will do so when the time comes. And I will also seek political asylum and, mother, you must join me."

"How can you be so insolent? No respect. You have been here too long. Neither you nor I have any power to get your father out of jail." She then hesitated. "Well, we may have some but it is not great. It is up to the government; they have all the cards in their hands. We are going back as soon as our visa runs out, and that is that! " Mother got up and left the room.

After a few minutes of painful silence, she returned.

"Gentlemen, I am very sorry about all this. I think the wine did this to her. She will be all right tomorrow. Please do not let this reflect on our hospitality and on your generosity in helping us to become happy in your country. You have been very good to us. We have enjoyed our stay here very much and my daughter has learned much at your university.

Yes, her father is in difficulty, but we can deal with that better at home. We have contacts there. Staying here will just make the situation worse. Please understand me."

"Of course, we understand," William quickly responded. "We will do everything to help you, although I am not sure what we can do about your husband. That seems to be totally in the hands of your government." Almost imploring, he looked at Richard. "Right?"

"Right."

Student looked at both with a mixed expression of embarrassment and defiance. "You do not know me, nor my people. We do not give up easily. I have thought this over for a long time. I like the U.S., but not totally. Many, many Americans are too concerned with money and having fun, but I can see why. There are great riches here and why not take advantage of them? I like very much living comfortably with my mother here in a nice apartment, not having to worry about the police and all that stuff. I am sure you know what I am talking about. But my country and my people have to be helped from the outside. They are too cowed and restrained by their own government to do anything."

She stopped to catch her breath. "But it is not totally our government's fault. We are a small and weak country and many outsiders who are larger and stronger than us want our land. You probably do not know what this means, but I am sure your Native Americans know what I mean. My hope is that some powerful country that understands us will help us. Your country has this power. 'Might for right,' someone once said to me. I hope your country will use might for right."

"Stop, stop! You have said enough," Mother raised her voice again. "You will never succeed, and in the meantime your father will remain in jail. One way or another, we must work at home to convince our authorities to let him out."

"Okay, okay," Richard said and walked over to Mother. "We are very grateful for your invitation, and we understand both of you. Now we must go. I only wish you will do nothing drastic, and we would be grateful if you contact us whenever you feel like it." He wanted to tell them his plans before their visit ended. "Oh, yes, I must mention: I will be going back to your country within the month to finish my project."

William looked up in amazement.

"I just got a letter from your district minister of culture inviting me and I am very grateful to him. Now, I would be very grateful if you gave me permission to talk to him about your situation. I will tell him what you want me to tell him. but only if you want me to." He reached his hand toward Mother. "Can you at least give me the chance to do that?"

She looked at him curiously. "Perhaps."

"But I don't want this to have international consequences. I could try to convince them to release your husband, but then . . . " Richard wished he had not gone so far. William stared at him without expression. Richard knew that was his way of masking his disapproval.

William got up and stretched out his hand to Mother. "Goodbye and many thanks for your wonderful hospitality." He turned to Student, "Goodbye to you, too, and thank you." He went to the door with Richard sheepishly following.

On the way back to the university William and Richard said nothing. Since their favorite coffee shop was on the way, they walked into it automatically and headed for their table against the wall in the back. They ordered coffee.

"Whew!" Richard looked at William. "Now what?"

"Well, as we in intelligence would call them, they are most likely sleepers used to penetrate a target country and appear as reliable, honest people seeking new citizenship. They study, work hard at honest jobs. get settled, and then sometime—they never know when—they will get the call to help their country. Many of them are good people but are compelled to do what they are told—frequently they do it to keep someone back home from getting into trouble. Blackmail. You know all about this."

"Come on," Richard said. "What would a small country do with such an arrangement? If it were discovered, they could have serious problems— trade embargo, loss of international standing. Who knows—just for some piddling amount of information obtained by two amateur spies?"

"We don't know. We are living in different times since our great disaster. Those who perpetrated the attack last year did not represent a super power. Well, I must head back. We'll keep in touch." William got up to leave, but then turned to Richard.

"Oh, yes. We should come up with something before you leave for their country. By the way, I did not know you got such an invitation."

"I did." (he is really miffed) "It's the only chance for me to test my theory and complete my research plan."

"I understand. The problem now is figuring out how to help these ladies—if we should or could—by working something out with the minister of culture. I hope we can discuss this soon. As for Mr. Security, it's too premature to say anything about it to him. Besides, he may know much more than we do, and the less we know, the better. I'm sure you learned that in intelligence. Knowing absolutely nothing about something means you can't say anything useful to interrogators. However, then you must come up with a credible fiction. The problem is, good interrogators figure that out pretty quickly. Cheerio."

William was a bit triumphant as he walked through the cigarette haze toward the door, coughing loudly in disapproval.

Richard watched him, then fell into deep thought. He put his head down and closed his eyes. The dinner and the discussion after it were getting to him. (now what . . . what am I going to say to Mr. Minister of Culture . . . ? that rat . . . he must have asked others to do what I ended up doing . . . he knew I was a softy . . . I talked too much about cooperation . . . ha, ha . . . joke's on me . . . always something new to learn in life . . . but why go back . . . ? don't answer his letter . . . let him stew . . . especially when he finds out about Student . . . but then my videotapes and Student's father . . . must think this one out very carefully)

Richard got up and slowly walked through the cafe looking at the students there. (all these innocent young people, relaxed, unencumbered by such life-challenging problems . . . are they smarter than all of us old guys who claim to have learned something over the years, or just lucky?)

Richard spent the whole evening mulling over the invitation.

(basta . . .I'm going). He called William and asked him to meet at the café for lunch.

During lunch the next day, William read the invitation. While he read, Richard watched him. (aha . . . he's still surprised but won't show it)

"Richard, this is a very interesting invitation. You may be able—I say 'may'—to carry out your research plan without any difficulty, but I have several questions: do you really think you can carry out your plan in a scientifically respectable way? And can their government ensure your safety? Not only are armed people running around over there, but normally friendly citizens may not be trustworthy. In uncertain times strangers are usually viewed as spies and things can get very rough. And last of all, the minister of culture—can you trust him? Working as an airport customs official means he very likely also works for state intelligence. No, no, it looks like a trap. Richard, I would not answer his letter. You are of far greater value to humanity if you stay here."

Richard smiled and looked at William. "You really feel strongly about this."

"Don't get sarcastic."

"Okay, I know there are problems, but when am I going to have a chance to see that country again? It's fascinating—the people, the landscape. The schools were good to me and I am sure they will be especially nice because their government is behind me. Besides, I have to try out my method for educating kids to cooperate. That's the best I can do with my limitations to make a contribution."

"Okay, okay, you made your point. I still hope you will give this serious thought before making a final decision."

"I will, I will."

10

EXPLANATIONS

THE DAY BEFORE EMBARKING on his trip to conclude his year-long study, Richard stopped by William's office.

"I'm off tomorrow to you know where. Any final words?"

"Plenty. Richard, we don't know these people. Most of them may be okay, but some may be dangerous. Yes, I know working with their children guarantees some degree of protection that you won't be arrested or anything like that. I agree, anyone concerned about their children can't be that dangerous an enemy. Unless, of course, that person is doing something unacceptable."

"Right. I am an acceptable, clean guy."

"Wrong. You are not totally clean. Remember, you did tape on-ground scenes in addition to the school children in your research. The minister of culture must know that by now."

"It's possible he hasn't see those shots. Actually, I should say, I don't think he has seen those shots. I obviously can't prove it."

"Why would you ever think that?"

"He wrote in his letter that he looked at a few minutes of my video clips of the children playing with the Fun-Cartoon Machine and was bored. I don't blame him. They are interesting only to me and other scientists. He most likely never saw those other shots."

"Richard, unless you're sure, you know you can't take chances."

"But if he did see them, why wouldn't he see it as a harmless tourist kind of thing? Here's this guy, riding a bus and taking video shots of his surroundings. No, I think you are too paranoid about this."

"Could be, but . . . "

William's secretary knocked on his office door. "A visitor."

"Okay, Richard, good luck and come back safely." As William got up to shake Richard's hand, the visitor suddenly came into the room.

"Surprise! Your friendly security guy."

"I'll be. It's Mr. Security! (what a coincidence) "Well, I'll excuse my-self gentlemen." Richard headed for the door.

"No, no. Please stay," Mr. Security said. "This meeting is mainly about you, Professor Richard."

"Oh!" (why me?)

"Actually, I came especially to see you." He looked at Richard smiling. "But you were not in your office so I came here to find out if you, Professor William, knew where he was."

"Here I am."

"Let me get right down to business. Professor Richard, I recall you told me some time back that you may be returning to the country where you did the video research with children."

"Yes." (this guy keeps track . . . he really wants those videotapes)

"Well, I was just routinely checking visas for this country and there was your name. You know this country is currently in deep trouble A dissident group—some call them bandits, others patriots, still others rebels, insurrectionists, and whatever the government wants to call them—is massing in the south of the country. Its force is small but growing, so you may be caught up in something that could put you in danger."

"I was trying to tell him this," William said with satisfaction.

"Now, if you still plan to go, our government wants to make sure you have the best protection we can give you as an American citizen."

"Yes." (how in the world are they going to be able to do that?)

"The best way we can do that at this moment is by using this." Mr. Security pulled an envelope out of his pocket and removed a plastic card, about four millimeters thick.

"This is a simple radio transmitter. I say 'simple' because all it transmits is a beep. When activated—it can be activated once and only once—it will emit an inaudible beep once every five minutes. This beep can be picked up by a receiver within an approximately thirty-kilometer radius. We already have several of these receivers in reconnaissance planes over that country. I'm sure you know this is all top secret. Anyway, keep this card along with your passport. We recommend putting it with your passport in your chest pouch. It has a rubber band around it so you don't inadvertently pull it out when they ask for your passport. On one side, the card looks like a life insurance card, on the other like a medical insurance card. As you can see, both look very authentic. If you are in trouble, fold the card and break its back to stop the beeping. The absence of this beep will signal that you are in trouble, and our interpreter center will then determine your location and send that information to our rescue team. Appropriate action will then be taken to assist you. It's as simple as that."

"Impressive." (really . . . will it work?)

"Richard," William said. "If you still plan to get on that plane, I ask you as an old friend to take it. It may save your life."

"And if whoever it is that doesn't like me finds this, then what?"

"They shouldn't get to it before you bend it. Most likely they will have no idea of its function. If you can't react quickly enough that could be problematic. We can't anticipate every possibility."

"I understand."

"Good. If you decide to take it with you, please pick it up from William on your way to the plane. He has instructions in this sealed envelope to activate the card. He will only activate the timer that turns on the beep when you are on the plane heading out of the U.S."

"Sounds like an ingenious plan, gentlemen, but I am only going there to work with children."

"Yes, but our policy is to take care of our citizens."

"I understand that and appreciate it. Thank you."

The next day on the way to the airport, Richard stopped in at William's office. "On my way, William, to pick up the card. You can activate it in about six or seven hours. My plane leaves in about two hours. See you when I get back."

As he left William's office there was another surprise. Student and Mother were waiting for him. "Oh! We're so glad to catch you. We came to say goodbye."

"Very nice of you." (did I tell them I was leaving today?)

"We have a request. We'd appreciate it very much if you took these letters to our friends." Student handed them to Richard. "You can give them to the minister of culture. He knows who our friends are."

"Oh, yes, and this one, too." Mother handed Richard a much larger sealed envelope.

"What is that, Mother?" Student looked perplexed.

Mother ignored her. "This is also for the minister of culture. He will be glad to have it."

"Okay, I'll put them right in here." Richard put the envelopes in his backpack. "It'll all work out. See you when I get back."

Mother looked at him closely. (trying to tell me something?)

"Come back safely," she murmured.

Once on the plane, Richard relaxed—temporarily. Something he promised himself some time ago came back to him. (I gotta stop doing this . . . but just once more . . . famous last words)

The flight was smooth—two stops, no excitement. His plans for research were all in his mind, ready to go. The plane landed and he felt relaxed and rested. He walked into the reception hall. (well, here again, same odors . . . same everything, but a few more armed personnel walking around . . . uh oh, here comes official number one)

"Passport please," the official asked.

"I am here to work in one of your schools," Richard said as he handed him the passport (already mistake one—never give any information without being asked for it). "I have a research permit." Richard gave him the letter from the minister of culture. (speak of the devil, here he is)

The minister looked a bit more disheveled and exhausted than last time. He smiled broadly and waved the official off. "Hello, Professor Richard. Good to see you again. It's been about a year. I hope you are still in good health."

"Yes, I am, thank you. Good to see you, too." (you snake) I never expected to see you again. But here we are, ready to pick up where we left off. Now what was it we were discussing?"

The minister smiled. "Somewhere in the middle of your explanation of why it is better to cooperate than fight. But let us go outside; the hotel is not far, so we will go there first, then take a walk. I always like to talk with colleagues while walking."

"Good idea." (no eavesdroppers)

Richard checked in the hotel, washed up a bit, then put the two envelopes into his shirt. He went to the lobby where the minister was waiting.

"Let's go," the minister said. "Stretching one's legs after a long flight is always a treat."

After they walked several blocks without talking, Richard turned to the minister. "Before I forget, this is for you from Student and her mother." He showed the minister the smaller of the two envelopes.

"Yes, yes, let's sit on that bench."

"These are letters for their friends." Richard gave him the smaller pack.

"Thank you. I will pass them on." He put them into his shirt.

"And this one is from her mother, for you." Richard handed him the larger envelope.

The minister weighed it in his hand. "She has lots to say." He then looked with a bit of curiosity at Richard. "You are a brave man."

Richard suppressed his surprise. "I don't think so. Why do you say so?"

"This." He held up the envelope.

"Is there something in there that could get me in trouble?"

"Very much so. Trouble from your own people if they found you with it. But I figured they would not check you on departure. It is a somewhat long story, but you should hear it now. Let us walk a bit down this street to that building site over there."

"Okay." (must be something pretty important)

"Mother's husband and I were very good friends from way back. He was an excellent scholar and commentator on political matters. Alas, he was too outspoken against our government's policies—despite warnings from me and others. He was arrested several times and then released. However, about two years ago he was jailed indefinitely. Getting him released was virtually impossible. Anyone associated with a prisoner is always suspect, so it was unsafe to even show interest in his situation. To make a long story short, I concocted a plan to help him and—don't be shocked—you became part of it. My plan was to promise the higher ups that my daily contact with foreigners made it possible for me to establish contacts in the U.S. and to get some on-the-ground intelligence information. My plan was to recruit visitors who seemed kind enough to sponsor a student in the U.S. After about six or seven tries, I succeeded with you. Does that make you feel special?" He smiled.

Richard held his breath. (you b . . . s . . . t . . . rd)

"Sorry, but you most likely would have done the same to save a friend. Anyway, you were a perfect choice since you were a faculty member at a prominent university situated on one of America's great rivers. And the kind of information? Our government wants to know everything about the bridges that span that river. Why? I leave that up to your imagination."

"Yes, I can imagine. The U.S. has become a target of quite determined enemies."

"Precisely. Releasing my dear friend from prison was contingent on any information I could supply on U.S. infrastructure—your bridges were my choice for reasons that will become clear. This information had to be obtained by some reliable person. My friend's wife, Student's mother, could not be more reliable."

"Does Student know about this?"

"Student knows nothing about it. The fewer in on a plan, the better. And I am pretty sure her mother kept silent about it. Too much is at stake."

"Okay, but I still don't understand all this."

"Now, let us go over behind that wall and I will have a smoke."

They casually went around the wall, which was about waist high. (an ideal spot . . . a passerby could probably see someone having a smoke there and not become suspicious)

"Now let us see what Mother has provided us." The minister opened the envelope and pulled out a sheaf of papers. "I see no one has opened this envelope unless they were very skillful—which I doubt has been the case. Ah, hah! Sketches of bridges—two big ones. Those two really got around."

"Student's sketches," whispered Richard.

"And many notes on their structural features and materials—steel, concrete, alloys used in cables, joints, minute fracture lines, rivets per meter, and so on and so on. You see, Mother always wanted to be an engineer, and she was perfect for this job for three reasons: she could update her knowledge of bridge materials, her daughter was interested in architecture, and her husband's fate rested in her hands. If someone got suspicious of them, Mother, could talk her away around it, and I am sure she would not reveal anything significant. She is a very bright and savvy person. Also, I am sure it never occurred to her that the information she collected would be used for unfriendly purposes. My guess is she thought that such information would help us to construct better bridges. Student could not talk since she knows nothing about it. So all we had to do is get both of them into the U.S."

(you snake)

"Don't be surprised. Can you remember? You said to me that to get the truth about something, one has to cross borders to find it—even if it was a bit tricky or dangerous at times. That is my idea as well," he chuckled. "I wonder whether Student and her mother learned anything new crossing your border."

Richard tried to suppress his anger. "Probably, but let me stick to the issue. I am glad you understand my idea about crossing borders. That pleases me. But let us get to Student and Mother. What future do they have?"

"I'm not sure. But no one need know they have done this. Of course, they—and you—would have been in deep trouble if you had been stopped and inquiries were made about the contents of this envelope. Now, as it stands, only two of us know, in this country at least."

"Uh, oh. I don't understand." A sudden panic stabbed Richard. "What happens to me now?"

"Sir, don't panic."

"How could I have been so naive?"

"That's easy. If you live in a safe and comfortable environment, as most of you in the U.S. do, it is easy to become naive."

"Yes, but . . . "

"Allow me to finish. There is a very painful part of to all of this.

My dear friend, Student's father, was found dead in his cell three days ago. The authorities said it was a heart attack. I am still stunned, although, I knew he had a bad heart. My guess is they will do an autopsy and, if it is true that he died of an unexpected heart attack, they will publicize it widely. If he was tortured to death, they will still publicize it as an unexpected heart attack. You see, when you control the channels of information, the truth can be anything you want."

Richard reached for the envelope, but the minister pulled it away.

"Don't be impetuous," the minister said. (you b . . . st . . . rd) "As my very new friend, would you please light my cigarette?" He put the envelope under his left arm. Richard watched it. (next time I'll get it)

The minister gave Richard his lighter, took out a cigarette, and put it between his lips. "We are friends? Right? Give me a light, please."

Richard lit his cigarette. (the envelope is still too far to reach)

"Good. You are a good man." The minister inhaled deeply. "Now do me the honors." He spread out several of the drawings into a fan. Give them some fire."

Richard looked at him, hesitated a moment (aha), then smiled. "Good idea." He put the flame to their edges.

"Excellent." the minister spread the drawings out, letting the flames engulf each page. The curling pieces fell to ground. "Now let us continue with more fire." He repeated this with all the drawings along with the pages of Mother's notes. A small pile of burning paper collected at his feet.

Richard watched intently. He handed the lighter back to the minister, who seemed mesmerized by the fire. Then Richard pulled out his chest pouch, removed his 'insurance card,' and dropped it on the burning pile.

The minister looked at him. "I hope that wasn't your passport."

"No."

In a few minutes the pile was reduced to ashes. The card crackled a bit. (and so it goes)

The minister stood up and stomped the pile into the earth. "That should do it." He stared at it for a minute. "This is the end we all face."

Richard did not move.

"Now let us get to the future. First, a drink; I need one badly."

They resumed their walk in silence. "Mr. Richard, you still have your project to carry out."

"Yes." Richard was a bit surprised he still had any interest in his project.

"I have made arrangements for you at the school. They are delighted you are coming back. Excuse me, but I hope you have a bit of you-know-what for them. Teachers are not well paid here. They will give you a small room where they store their school records. It should do, especially if you don't like sleeping in big spaces like classrooms." He chuckled. "You can eat your meals with the teachers. Payment for the accommodations and food will be greatly appreciated. I guess that's it." The minister took a last drag from the cigarette.

"Oh, one more thing—a bit disturbing. Our country is becoming increasingly unstable. A group of armed men to the south of us—about 150 kilometers from here—is slowly gathering forces and moving in our direction. Our military units are already deployed and will engage them before long. I think these men can be defeated, but rumor has it they are growing everyday—many disaffected people in the south—crops have failed because they have had no rain for several years now."

"I can understand. People have to eat. Your government must help them. If the government runs out of money it can borrow it and tax the farmers later."

The minister ignored him. "I mention this because if they enter this area, you may be in danger. They will detain all foreigners and who knows what will happen then. In any case, I have discussed this possibility and the teachers will get to you to a place in some hills north of the city. The people there will take care of you until all this blows over. That's the best I can do for now."

"Thank you."

"Oh, yes, if I do not see you again, I'd appreciate it if you convince Student and Mother to seek political asylum in the U.S. By the time you return, they will most likely be informed of their loved one's fate, so you will be spared informing them of that. His death will strengthen their case for asylum."

"And you," Richard said. "What about you? What about that pile of ashes back there? Sooner or later, someone will ask about your bridge plan with Mother. Then the ax will fall on your head."

"Thank you for your concern, but I don't know what you are talking about. Ha, ha. No matter what, I will stay here. My failure in the bridge plan will not become an issue for some time—the authorities will be too preoccupied with that group in the south. Anyway, this is my country—for better or worse. I will stay with it no matter what. I am sure you understand that."

"I do."

They shook hands and parted.

Back in his hotel room, Richard suddenly remembered the minister did not have his drink. He also remembered he failed to ask the minister about the videotapes.

11

MISSION ACCOMPLISHED?

THE NEXT DAY TWO teachers came to pick Richard up at the hotel. Their meeting was the happiest thing that he experienced since his arrival, which wasn't much, but under the circumstances . . .

He was given his 'room' in the rear of the school—a cot between big shelves of musty, gray folders, a small table holding a candle and some matches, and a door that could be latched with a hook and eye from the inside. He checked the outside of the door and found two small holes where the hook and eye were originally located. (at least they can't lock me in from the outside, and if the bandits come, I'll be safe . . . ha, ha)

After an ample meal of local whatever it was, they all drank green tea and relaxed. "We're glad you came back," one teacher said. "The children were told you were coming. A few of them remember. About half of them you met last time are still here in school. The others have left to work."

"Work? They should stay in school! They are too young to work."

"Many of them who are no longer here are girls, but now more and more boys are also leaving school to work."

"Why? They should stay here and get an education. They can work later, the rest of their lives."

"We all know that, but these are very hard times and those who do not work do not eat."

The following day he went to the classroom with a small bag containing his equipment. Some children were smiling and two were clapping. (now the clown will perform)

He bowed in jest. He then pulled out of his bag a small, hand-held plastic viewer with a two-inch crank and inserted a cartoon cartridge into it. He held up the viewer and looking into it, turned the crank, and then began laughing. "I see funny things here. Ha, ha! It's Mickey Mouse. You know Mickey Mouse?"

"Let me see, let me see!" Many hands reached for it.

"Wait. It is time to take turns. If you don't take turns, no one will see it, then you will feel sad. Maybe some of you will even get into a fight."

Some seemed to be satisfied with his answer, others not.

Richard held his breath. "Okay, let's give it to the smallest person in this room. Who is it? They all pointed to a girl in the middle row.

"She is the smallest because her legs are crooked," a child yelled out.

Richard motioned to her. "Please come up here."

The girl shyly went up to him. Richard looked at her (poor nutrition). "Now you can see Mickey Mouse." She took the viewer and turned the crank forward, then backward, then forward again. Some of the children laughed. She continued for two minutes.

"Okay, now we must let someone else have it." Richard reached for it, but she held on to it, moving away from him and continuing to crank furiously. She was dead serious. (now what, big genius?)

The whole class began laughing.

She kept turning, grimly and with increasing vigor. "Unfair, unfair!" someone cried out. Richard moved toward her and she slipped behind the teacher's desk. Again great laughter. (God this is becoming a disaster?)

Richard then stepped forcefully toward the class. "Quiet! I have a question for you. Forget her. Do not look at her, look at me. Listen to my question. See, she is having fun with Mickey Mouse. Why shouldn't we give her a bit more time to see him?"

"Because then we won't be able to see him."

"Why didn't you bring more Mickey Mouse machines?"

"Because I have only one machine."

"You should have brought more with you."

From the back of the room, a boy yelled loudly. "It is not his fault!" (thank you greatly)

"We waited long enough." A tall boy got out of his seat and started toward the girl. "It is my turn now."

"Whoa! No, you won't." Richard walked quickly toward the boy. On the way, someone tripped him. He stumbled. Great laughter.

The girl stopped turning the lever, went over to Richard, and with absolutely no expression on her face, gave it to him as he was getting off the floor. Richard took it from her. "Thank you, thank you."

The room suddenly became silent. He wondered why. The class was looking at someone behind him. The head teacher was standing in the door. "Class dismissed!"

The children got up and ran out, talking and laughing. Others left somewhat subdued.

The head teacher looked at Richard. "These are things we have to expect. The children want more excitement; they want to learn new things. Look, they don't have enough books. Many of them are bored and angry. As they experience this day after day, they get restless and angry and begin to disobey their parents and us. The boys more than the girls. And Mr. Richard, do you know what many of these boys will be doing a few years from now?"

"I can imagine."

"Can you really imagine? They will run away and become soldiers. They will be given part of a uniform and more food to eat. They will also be mistreated for a while to make them angry. And then they will be given a gun. Then . . . "

"Yes, I know."

"This was an unpleasant experience for you and we are sorry."

"Of course. No need to feel sorry. I just have more to learn."

"Will you come back tomorrow?"

"Of course. I have already learned a few lessons. Now I will try something else."

"Good." she smiled. "Now let us go to the kitchen for a mid-morning tea."

The next day, Richard quickly estimated that the class had grown a bit—five or six new faces. All seats filled and two sitting on the floor in the back. (interesting . . . they expect action)

"Good morning!"

"Good morning!" A few answered.

"Yesterday, Mickey Mouse got me in trouble."

Some children laughed.

"Today, I asked Mickey Mouse if he would let me invite Donald Duck to help us play this game. Mickey said 'Yes.'"

The class was not impressed. "So I brought Donald here. Here he is." Richard inserted the Donald Duck cartridge into the viewer. Their interest picked up immediately.

"Now we have a Donald Duck in here. He is a funny duck. He is a new actor. Suppose I had many, many more funny animals like him. Wouldn't that be nice? I have two more but not with me today."

"Yes, we'd like a hundred more."

"Okay, but where would they come from? Someone has to make them."

"You make them."

"I can't. Do you know who has to make them?"

The room was silent.

"We can't!" a boy yelled in the back row.

"That's right. You can't make them because you don't have the tools and materials, but you can buy them. They are cheap."

"We have no money!"

"You have to work so you will have money."

"There is no work," the older boy in the back yelled out.

"You will be able to work if you get an education."

Silence.

"You can get an education if you work hard at your studies and share what you learn with your friends. You can get many good things. If you fight, you will never learn anything but how to fight and no one will ever see Mickey Mouse and Donald Duck."

Again, silence. (I doubt they got it)

"Can we see Donald Duck now?"

"Of course, but only if you share. Now, who will be the first one to see Donald Duck?"

Silence.

"Let that girl pick," the boy in the back row said. "She has seen Mickey Mouse and has had her fun." (genius . . . future Nobel Peace Prize winner)

"Good idea. Here. You give this to someone." Richard handed her the viewer.

She took it with a rare expression on her face, looked around, and gave it to the girl sitting next to her.

After the girl cranked about a minute, she gave it to the boy behind her. (God . . . oh God . . . progress is possible)

By the end of 45 minutes, most of the class had seen Donald Duck.

After a ten-minute break when the children ran out to play, they returned to the classroom for their reading class.

Richard enjoyed his mid-morning tea. (now for tomorrow)

In several days, all four cartoons were cranked out, with Richard inserting his lectures about sharing, cooperating, avoiding fighting. (it sounds pretty preachy . . . but why not?)

"What else can I do," he asked the head teacher after class.

She thought awhile. "Not much, but repetition is good. Of course, they eventually will get bored and after you leave, many other things they learn in school (and life) will take over their minds. But repetition can lay down a strong memory trace, and novelty can too. You and Mickey Mouse are novel."

(I made it . . . finally . . . at least a bit)

Richard smiled. "Yes, but . . . but I hope one thing. I hope that the novelty of all this will also help them to remember the message of sharing."

"That could happen."

Richard moved to another class.

When he later returned to the first class he had a new idea (this may be pushing it). He was going to ask them a question.

"Okay class, I have a question for you. Suppose a big man came in here and said, 'Sharing is no good. Sharing is for sissies. The only way you can get to see Mickey Mouse is to fight to see him.

Fighting is the best thing to do, don't share.' Now who of you believes this man is right and should fight?"

Silence.

Restlessness.

"Come, come, you must give me an answer."

More silence.

"Okay. Those of you who think he is right, raise your hand."

Three boys and one girl raised their hands.

"Why is he right?"

One boy muttered something.

"What did you say?"

Another child said loudly, "He said the man was right. Everybody fights and if you don't fight you will never see Mickey Mouse."

"Suppose you fight and lose?"

"You don't fight unless you can win. Everybody knows that."

Laughter.

And so it went—pulling teeth to get an answer. Absolutely no consensus. Class dismissed. (should have known that would happen . . . at least I tried)

12

LAST BORDER

THE NEXT DAY RICHARD was unexpectedly awakened by a knock on his door before sunrise.

"You must leave immediately. The bandits are coming close to the city. You can no longer stay. We are sorry. Our janitor will take you to a distant place. He comes from there. Tell no one. Not even the teachers."

Richard got up and hastily wrote a note to the head teacher. "Thanks for your kind hospitality. Must go. Keep the video machine and the cassettes, and give my personal things to who ever needs them. Hope to see you again some day."

It was 3 A.M. Five minutes later Richard found himself sitting behind the janitor on a rattling motorcycle, holding on for life (what the hell . . . nothing like seeing a country first hand). He felt anxious and exhilarated.

After about an hour and a half, mostly uphill, his driver stopped and turned to Richard. "I see dust up ahead. We can't stay here."

He turned off the road, drove through a grove of stunted trees, and headed toward a pile of rubble. (looks like a small village, or used to be)

"We will stay here awhile." His driver parked his bike behind a fallen wall.

They stayed the whole morning and into early afternoon. The driver scanned the road—forward and behind. "Okay, let's go."

After another hour, he yelled back to Richard, "We are almost there. Are you all right?"

"Yes. The sky is beautiful."

"Yes, this is a beautiful country. We all love it here."

After another ten minutes, the driver turned off on a very rough steep road for about thirty yards and stopped. "This is it. Too steep. We must walk from here."

A rough trail ran over a rocky talus slope with soft, shallow valleys. After about fifteen minutes, they approached a cluster of huts.

"We stay here in the summer with flocks. The grass is good here. Because winter is coming most of those staying here have left. The others will soon leave. As for you, you will be safe here—I think. Our grandmother will stay here with you."

Richard noticed her standing with the others. "That is very kind of her." He then pulled out his wallet. The driver ignored it.

"She will stay here no matter what. She is stubborn about leaving this place. She was born near here and has never left."

"This is for you and for her and the others." He took out his money, except the five twenty-dollar bills zipped into his money belt, and handed it to him. "We may need some food after awhile so I would appreciate it if you brought us something to eat—when it is not dangerous. Keep the rest."

"Thank you, sir, thank you so much."

"One question." Richard turned again to the driver. "Do people around here know that grandmother stays here during the winter months?"

"Yes, but mostly only relatives in the town nearby who take her food and check up on her."

"What about dogs? I see no dogs here."

"We already took them down—except for one. He will stay here with grandmother. He is old but can bark well and listens only to her. He is probably sleeping."

"Good. You know it is very important that no one knows I am up here."

"Of course. We know about these things. Many things have happened in this valley over history. Invaders and tax collectors have come here many, many times, and we always outfox them. Ha, ha."

"Oh, yes, one more question: does grandmother have a gun?"

His driver smiled. "Yes, an old one. I don't think she ever uses it. If you plan to use it, you better check it out first."

As they reached the huts, the grandmother and four young men stopped their lively conversation to regard the approaching stranger.

One man who was holding a rifle discreetly set it against a hut, then clambered effortlessly onto the roof and started scanning the valley. (good move)

"Hello!" Richard smiled.

They looked at him. Several nodded.

The driver went over to them and carried on a lengthy conversation. Richard could only catch a few words of what they were saying. He turned to look at the valley's breathtaking view. (how many travelers have seen this)

On the mountain behind him was a long steep hill of rock strewn fields with patches of grass stubble. The hill rose gradually toward a vast area of dolomite gullies and ridges—glacier run-off erosion. (a hundred places to hide . . . and get trapped . . . but mountain people have never lost a war . . . for long)

Snowflakes suddenly drifted on to his face. He opened his mouth and tried to catch them. (Uh oh . . . that is good . . . it will deter visitors.) Far off, he heard a wolf howl. A chill ran up his neck.

The driver came back to Richard. "They understand what to do. Some are worried about grandmother. The bandits may harm her, but she won't leave."

Richard looked at her, nodded, and smiled. She looked back at him cautiously. (at least she doesn't fear me . . . why, why do I always run into nice grandmothers . . . she is one of the eternal ones)

Suddenly a man came running down from the hill out of breath. They greeted him effusively. He had come straight from the school on a truck by way of a distant pass and had gone by foot about two kilometers. He spoke rapidly to the others, then looked at Richard and smiled.

The motorcycle driver saw him smile and turned to Richard, "He is the brother of the head teacher. I am sure she told him about you—-some of the children did too."

"Oh, I hope it was not too negative."

"No, no. It was positive. They said you tried hard to teach them important things, but were not sure you succeeded." He laughed.

"But they appreciated that you tried and they like the toys you left behind."

"Good!" Richard gave the man thumbs up. The man smiled broadly.

Suddenly, the man on the roof yelled something. The others looked at each other in alarm. The driver pushed Richard against the wall of the nearby hut. "They have seen my bike."

A truck with armed men stopped on the road below. Two got out carrying weapons. They walked over to the bike, then stared farther up the hill. They went back to the truck and were joined by a third soldier.

"They will be over that rise in about five minutes," the driver said to Richard. "You cannot stay here. They will search the huts. You must go up there." He pointed to the hill.

The brother of the head teacher approached Richard, "It is not good if you stay here long—word gets out. If you keep going straight ahead, in about an hour you will get to the pass. On the other side of the pass is a border. You won't see it, but it is about 150 meters below the ridge. You will be safe there."

"Wow!" Richard was astonished at the speed of their decisions. "But how can I go straight ahead? There are many gullies up there. How do I find the right one?"

"There are many that are small enough to climb out of if you get to the end of them. Finding the right ones is mostly luck. You will learn which is the right one because the wrong ones come to an end. Sorry, I can tell you no more."

"Okay. I will try my best." (no sense in pushing . . . they've made up their minds . . . too dangerous if I stay around) Richard pulled up his jacket collar. (gloves . . . why didn't I bring gloves . . . ? William . . . William you were right)

He turned to the others. "Thank you. You are kind to help me."

The grandmother removed her shawl and handed it to Richard.

"Oh, my!" Richard took it from her and automatically brought his hands together as if in prayer. "Namaste."

She smiled. "Namaste."

He wrapped the shawl around his neck, fastening it in a big knot. He turned around and waved. (now to get out of here without being seen)

After about five minutes in a part run, he remembered the soldiers and threw himself to the ground. He then crept on his stomach to a large rock and wiggled his way behind it. He looked down at the huts. In a few minutes the soldiers appeared. His driver went to greet them and shook hands with the man who seemed to be their leader. The other two soldiers moved toward the huts with their rifles half-raised. One soldier went inside the first hut while the other stood outside watching. After they checked all four huts, they went to their leader and nodded.

The brother of the head teacher went into a hut and came out carrying a bottle. He passed it around. It must have been schnaps. Richard heard faint laughter. (they are enjoying themselves . . . good)

The three soldiers turned around and proceeded down the hill. Richard waited until they were completely out of sight before getting up. He was already stiff. (walking will get me warm)

After about fifteen minutes, the winds picked up and the snow began falling faster and thicker (uh oh . . . this is not going to be good). He pulled the shawl tighter around his neck and buried his face in it. (God bless her)

The walking got harder as the snow began piling up (gotta stop . . . gotta rest). He sat down (no . . . no . . . don't sit down . . . keep moving), got up, and walked a few steps. (oh no)

He sat again for a while, feeling very comfortable (rest a bit . . . no . . . can't rest long). Then he heard what sounded like a wolf calling (oh no . . . must be the wind). He listened very closely, trying to pick the call out of the wind. He didn't hear it again. (good . . . not a wolf . . . but must keep moving)

He tried to get up but fell back. He looked back toward the huts, which were now concealed by clouds of blowing snow. And then he saw it—something black moving in his direction. (oh no . . . God have mercy . . . Christ have mer . . .) Then it disappeared.

13

REVELATIONS

"WILLIAM HERE: I AM at a loss for words. For the first time since I've known Richard I have completely lost track of him. He was to call the day of his departure after completing his teaching program. That was days ago. To make matters worse, Mr. Security just informed me his office also lost contact with him.

As you know, I told Richard his journey was risky given that country's instability and its grievances against foreigners intervening in internal affairs. I am sure he was aware that in uncertain times, danger increases the farther one travels from home. Really, but what can one do if the authorities suspect one is a criminal or spy? Sneak over a border in a truck under a pile of watermelons, swim across a river a night? What are one's chances then?

What can I say now? I am at a loss to explain why he felt he had to take such chances. He and I always agree on the need to respect people, work for the welfare of everyone (especially children), fight for justice, and keep searching for the truth—all those activities that constitute civilized living.

But . . . but we differed on several crucial issues. One core belief that separated us was the notion that one individual can change the bigger state of things. What really change human behavior, as I see it, are wars, natural disasters—those factors beyond the control of an individual. Whether one survives or not is sheer luck.

As for Richard's research; interviewing people under stress is a weak method. What truth can you expect them to divulge?

Desperation not only clouds the mind and distorts memories, but also heightens paranoia so much that honesty is greatly compromised. Lying becomes a necessity when one is in danger.

As for educating school children—what a long and arduous process it is to change beliefs and behaviors! Such a process is frequently diluted or nullified by the individual personalities and conditions of the classrooms.

Hopefully, you will understand why I stay home in order to comment upon and make judgments of human activity. Civilization needs people to reflect on the major issues and not act unless it is with great judiciousness. The wilderness across the border can be barbaric and merciless.

Furthermore, it is not in my nature to try to change people's ways of life. As a professor, my job is to inform people, not to convince them to do things I think they should do. What right do I have to attempt to educate unwitting children about other people's problems? It seems patronizing and smacks of colonialism.

And what about recklessness? I can only do good if I am alive, and I can stay alive by minimizing risks. Now, what I'm going to say may sound horribly callous, but I must say it: I am here. Richard is not. He took too many risks. He was for life. I am for life. But I am alive, and he may already be dead.

Now I must make a confession. After I left intelligence work, as I noted earlier, I stayed in contact over the years with the agency for which I worked. When Richard applied for a visa for his first research trip—with his Fun-Cartoon Machine—I informed our old intelligence agency because I was worried about Richard's safety. That resulted in the gentleman —we came to call him Mr. Security—coming to talk to Richard.

My guess is that at first Mr. Security wasn't too concerned about Richard's safety. Most likely, he saw Richard as a way to collect first-hand information on a country that conceivably could become an enemy of the U.S. As you must know, information gathering is practiced by every country—even during peacetime.

When Richard's videotapes were confiscated, Mr. Security became concerned. He wanted no foreign incident if the country got a hold of the tapes and concluded that Richard was a spy.

When Richard later said he was going back to the country, Mr. Security became especially concerned. If Richard was suspected by that country—for whatever reason—the consequences could be disastrous for the U.S.—even if he were totally innocent—which, in a sense, he was not, given his taping of sites with possible intelligence value. Getting those tapes back became Mr. Security's top priority.

Mr. Security tried to control the situation by keeping track of Richard. Ergo, his tracking device—the 'insurance card' that beeps every five minutes.

Now comes the inexplicable part (for me, at least). According to Mr. Security—as you already know—if Richard got into trouble he was to bend the card and the beeping would cease, thereby alerting our reconnaissance unit to send out a rescue team.

The other night it occurred to me: how could any group rescue Richard in such a country without causing an international incident? Let's face it: Richard's tapes most likely do not have high intelligence value. Could the agency be so stupid? I doubt it.

Then, then . . . it dawned on me. Suppose, just suppose, Richard was caught because they suspected he was a spy and he decided to de-activate his beeper. Just suppose—I'm loathe to say it—when the card was bent—here's where it becomes horrendous—it exploded. No easily identifiable person, no specific country to blame for espionage, no clear explanation for anything.

God, why didn't I think that could have been a possibility before I activated the card? No, no, no. We would never do that to one of our own . . . or would we in the name of national security? Is not the fate of the common good of far greater importance than the fate of any individual? But not only that . . . excuse me. That phone won't stop ringing.

Hello. Yes, this is William. Could you speak louder, please? Uh oh! The phone just went dead." William stood up nervously.

"As I was saying. Where was I? Oh yes, national security.

Yes, the common good takes precedence over the good of the individual citizen. If that were not the case, no society could survive for long.

Oh, there goes that phone again.

Hello. Can you speak louder, please?"

"Is this Professor William?"

"Yes."

"Richard is on his way home."

"What? What? Who is this?"

"The district minister of culture—you know, from that country you feel so negative about. Ha, ha."

"Yes, yes. But . . . "

"I seem to be the one who specializes in getting your Richard out of our country. Ha, ha."

"Well, yes. Thank goodness he's all right. I thought he was in great danger and . . . "

"He was . . . for a while at least. But he has friends here."

"Friends?"

"I guess those mountain people got to like him. They found him in the snow on a hill, wrapped him up like a mummy, and tied him to a stretcher. Then they carried him down to the road. That's how the people up there get their sick to the hospital in the city. After they got him to the road, they got him on a truck all wrapped up—maybe he was with chickens—ha, ha. Anyway, instead of going to the hospital where he may have been recognized as a foreigner, they dropped him off here at the airport and brought him to my office. I know these people. It was very early in the morning and no one of importance was around except me. I recognized him immediately and took charge of him. He has a bit of frostbite on his hands and feet, but seems okay. He was quite exhausted. He had nothing with him other than his passport and plane ticket. No vital security stuff so we didn't have to detain him. Ha, ha. Oh yes, I gave him back his research tapes. You know, the ones he left here. They were boring and totally useless for any of our purposes."

"What? I thought . . . "

"Yes, yes, you thought we would arrest him for something or other, perhaps torture him a bit, and then put him up for ransom. Right? Some in our government may have done that, but that's not my style."

"Well, thank goodness for that, but"

"Come, come, sir. We don't hate every foreigner. In fact, we . . . no, I am running up a big phone bill here. Anyway, maybe some day we will have time and an opportunity to talk about all this in a quiet, civilized place. Goodbye."

"Wait! Wait! One question: did Richard say anything before he left?"

"Hmm, let me try to remember. Yes, he did, but I don't understand it. He said, 'If you contact William, tell him it's not all luck and lies.'"

www.ingramcontent.com/pod-product-compliance
Lightning Source LLC
Chambersburg PA
CBHW051145020726
47501CB00005B/1685